The ITALY Affair

University Chronicles Book 2

Ann Shepphird

The ITALY Affair

University Chronicles Book 2

4 Horsemen
Publications, Inc.

The Italy Affair
Copyright © 2024 Ann Shepphird. All rights reserved.

4 Horsemen
Publications, Inc.

Published By: 4 Horsemen Publications, Inc.

4 Horsemen Publications, Inc.
PO Box 417
Sylva, NC 28779
4horsemenpublications.com
info@4horsemenpublications.com

Cover & Typesetting by Autumn Skye
Edited by Jen Paquette

All rights to the work within are reserved to the author and publisher. No part of this publication may be reproduced, stored in a retrieval system, or transmitted in any form or by any means, electronic, mechanical, photocopying, recording, scanning, or otherwise, except as permitted under Section 107 or 108 of the 1976 International Copyright Act, without prior written permission except in brief quotations embodied in critical articles and reviews. Please contact either the Publisher or Author to gain permission.

All characters, organizations, and events portrayed in this novel are either products of the author's imagination or are used fictitiously.

All brands, quotes, and cited work respectfully belongs to the original rights holders and bear no affiliation to the authors or publisher.

Library of Congress Control Number: 2024941179

Paperback ISBN-13: 979-8-8232-0599-3
Hardcover ISBN-13: 979-8-8232-0600-6
Audiobook ISBN-13: 979-8-8232-0602-0
Ebook ISBN-13: 979-8-8232-0601-3

For Jeff

Chapter One
MAGGIE

Like many things in life, Italy was messier than I expected it to be. But here's what I learned: Messy isn't always a bad thing. Now, it may surprise you to hear that coming from me, someone who has made her living—her calling, even—bringing greater organization to the world. As an associate professor who teaches organizational communication at UC Berkeley, in addition to consulting with corporate boards on the topic, I like things to have clean, definable lines and work in an efficient manner. In fact, I have made it my mission in life to make that happen. I mean, proper organization really just makes everything easier, doesn't it? Especially when dealing with the incredibly messy entity that is the human being.

People. Ugh. If there is one thing I have learned in my study of people—especially when it comes to how they communicate with each other—it's that, well... Okay, I'm going to bottom line it for you here: people suck. There, I said it. I apologize for my bluntness, but it's true. Having studied the creatures for more than a dozen years now, it is my learned conclusion that (yes, I will say it again) people suck.

Now, I'm not saying this to justify myself after everything that happened in Italy. One never sets out to create an international incident, does one? I certainly didn't. But I do want to explain. And okay, this is not the first time I've had to explain (not justify!) myself. Four years ago, I created this thing called the War Council as a way to bring a little logic and, yes, organization to love. At the time, my theory was that if all is fair in love and war, why not have a little help on the battlefield? In the case of the War Council, that aid came in the form of a team of people with specific skill sets deployed to nudge the unsuspecting partners of our clients in the right direction. I envisioned the War Council team as similar to the squad in *Mission Impossible*, only for love. You know: *Your mission, Jim, should you choose to accept it, is to help these poor hapless souls get it together.*

I still feel the concept had validity, but in practice, not so much—especially when I found out that the War Council had been used behind my back to set up my relationship with Nick. When my first love Bill returned (talk about messy!), I realized just how manipulative the whole enterprise was, that love wasn't supposed to be logical, and I let the project run its course. Well, I did, anyway. My long-time friend Kathy, the Berkeley psychologist I recruited to be part of the project, ended up taking the War Council to a whole other level.

After my participation in the War Council ended, both the men in my life left Berkeley: Bill for a new job in New York and Nick for a planned year abroad in Paris. Then, in a bit of serendipity—or, I don't know, the universe fucking (excuse the French) with me a bit—I was offered a choice of two visiting lecturer positions as part of an academic sabbatical (not the rest-the-brain kind, the kind designed to "advance my knowledge base"). And get this: One of those positions was in New York and the other in Paris. Yep. New York and Paris. My relationships with Bill and Nick had both been left on positive terms and with the understanding that they could be picked up if we found ourselves in the same place again. That it was just timing or space or distance keeping us apart or whatever other bullshit we told ourselves. And here I was being offered the opportunity to take away that space and correct that timing with one of them. What are the odds, am I right? What kind of kismet was it that I was offered positions in the cities where the two men I had loved moved?

But here's the thing: The more I pondered it, the more I realized that I didn't want to take either position—at least not at that particular moment. Not only was I finally pretty darn happy in my own skin, but also why the hell did I have to go to either of them to make things work? Why did it feel like I had to do all the work? I didn't *have* to take either offer. So, I decided to table my sabbatical and instead take some time to advance my knowledge base in my own environment.

    I started by doing what any self-respecting academic in my situation would and wrote a treatise to process all that happened with the War Council, even though I couldn't use the name "War Council" because Kathy had copyrighted it. (Damn her!) Essentially, I dissected what the success of an organization that manipulated love using the paramilitary-style methods we created meant from a communication studies perspective. An academic book filled with all sorts of jargon, it also contained a modicum of humor. I may be an academic who loves organization, but that doesn't mean I checked my sense of humor at the door. Writing the book also helped justify the fact I had used school resources in my creation of the War Council. Luckily, the book was a hit, even with my department heads. (Hello! Points toward tenure!) I worried a bit about that as the Powers-That-Be sometimes frown on the addition of humor—not to mention using university resources to manipulate people's lives, even if (let's be honest) the psychology department does it all the time.

    On the flip side, writing the book put even more strain on what had become a rather fractured relationship with Kathy, who had been my best friend for a very long time (and I suppose still was on paper). The feeling of betrayal that came after she used the War Council behind my back to set me up with Nick, coupled with her insistence on continuing the enterprise, had created a distance between us. Kathy, the only member of the original team still involved with the War Council, was now serving as its CEO, even if the organization had been taken off campus after a particularly embarrassing incident involving a grad student and a dean.

It didn't help that I had Kathy constantly telling me that my decision to turn down those visiting lecturer positions came out of fear or resistance or some other psychobabble bullshit. (I mentioned she's a psychologist, right?) As I said, it was more that after all I'd been through with the War Council and reaching the ripe old age of 31, I was feeling good about myself and about staying in good ole Berkeley, not to mention using the clout I had accrued to continue advancing my career.

In the four years since, in addition to my burgeoning academic responsibilities, I had taken on some consulting work with a number of Bay Area organizations. I don't like to boast, but my superpower is the ability to walk into a room and immediately identify why a particular group might have trouble working well together. That's not to say there aren't groups where every piece of the puzzle fits, but they tend to be rare and not the case when I was hired to analyze them. Companies brought me in to pinpoint what had the potential to go (or already had gone) wrong. Now, many methodologies exist in this line of work, and I always added a bunch of academic-sounding jargon (metrics, analytics, test results, etc.) to make my reports look good. But the truth is, the minute I watched a group in action, I knew. I just knew. I could walk into a boardroom and know who would fill the role of the know-it-all or antagonist or passive-aggressive or overly aggressive or clown or suck-up. I, of course, used much more academic-sounding designations (or the personality types designated by letters and numbers that people seemed to love), but you get the drill. I was especially good at gleaning whether they lacked that special someone who just puts their head down and gets the job done, quite often the most challenging role organizations have to fill. It's kind of like putting on a play—while the actors and the director might get all the acclaim, it just ain't happening without the stage manager.

The most recent company I consulted with served as an excellent example: another tech company. The Bay Area was filled with them, and they often needed help, especially in the start-up stage. In general, tech people proved easier to analyze than those in other organizations. The people involved tended to communicate their roles in a more pronounced manner right away. Add in the fact they reeked of entitled superiority, and it made my job both easier and harder. With this particular company (name retracted per their NDA), instead of having me meet, test, and interview the various entities in their offices, they decided to have me observe the group as they participated in a "team-building exercise" at their company retreat. Ugh. Team building. Don't get me started. I'm not saying the concept doesn't have validity. Taking subjects out of their comfort zones through gamification can reveal much about personality types. That doesn't mean it wasn't excruciating to watch.

This particular group had hired a separate consultant to create a scavenger hunt (double ugh) through the expansive garden that surrounded the San Jose conference center they chose as their retreat site. I stood on the front porch of the center and watched the designated teams scurry through hedges and shimmy up trees looking for clues that told the history of the company and the product they were designing. As I dutifully noted the exhibited personality types, I found myself standing next to the consultant who had dreamed it all up. I gleaned this both from his conversation with the company CEO standing on the other side and the fact he wore a bright purple t-shirt with a "High-Intensity Team Building" logo across the chest that matched the purple tint on the tips of his blond hair.

"You the prof?" he finally said, turning to me and grinning like an idiot.

"I am the organizational communications consultant, yes."

"Cool beans."

"And you designed… this…" I said, waving my hand at the madness that was unfolding before us.

"Yes, it's called the Meet-the-Team Scavenger Hunt," he said with a manic energy and a tendency to sniff loudly that made me wonder what he was on. "This puppy is our most popular team-building exercise. It can be set up anywhere, from warehouses to office HQs to this rad garden they have here. We've franchised the concept to ten locations in the U.S. so far. Is this the best gig in the world or what?"

"Define what…"

Yeah, I know, total snark on my part. But you can see what I mean about people sucking, right? I had to deal with these folks on a regular basis, and I'll admit they tended to dampen my mood.

Once the "hunt" was over, the participants were treated to a cocktail-infused awards ceremony. I used the occasion to conduct a series of post-exercise interviews—the addition of the alcohol was quite helpful in loosening tongues. That completed, I had everything I needed (or could ever want), so I returned home, wrote up my analysis, and turned in a report with my conclusions about their team: what worked, what didn't, any deficits, etc. I then received a hefty little check in return. As I said, not bad work, and I was nicely compensated, but the more I dealt with these groups, the more I came to the aforementioned conclusion that people suck.

And in group environments, they really suck. Something about mixing it up in the Petri dish of humanity really brings out the worst in them.

I carried a bit of the grouchy mood that came out of that particular consulting gig with me as I arrived at Caffe Strada that fateful day in May when I received the Italy invitation. Even though we continued to have our issues and I barely saw her otherwise, Kathy and I still met at the same table every Thursday afternoon at 3 p.m. for a latte. Old habits die hard. Caffe Strada was located right off the UC Berkeley campus, an ideal location for both catching up and people-watching—Kathy eyeing potential new clients and me seeing them all as fodder for the "people suck" hypothesis I'd been bouncing around as a potential new avenue of research.

As usual, I arrived first. May I say that just once I would like for someone to already be waiting for me. I mean, it's not like I'm insanely early, although I am punctual. But that was never going to happen with Kathy. Miss "I'm so busy and important" Kathy never arrived on time, so I put in my order and then returned to our table to wait for her, my bad mood intensifying.

Once I had my latte, I sat back and looked around. As usual, a few students saw me and pointed to my picture on the back of my book about the War Council project: *Love Is Not*

Logical: The Case Against Manipulation in Relational Communications. One of my colleagues had chosen it for the introductory course on interpersonal communications. Good for book sales, not so much for maintaining anonymity on campus. The students grinned and waved, and I responded with a nod. I then saw Professor Gabriel, my colleague who taught political communications, sitting amid a gaggle of students with his Great Dane at his side. He took the beast, which was the size of a small horse, everywhere with him. A bit much, don't you think, to take your dog—a messy creature if there ever was one—everywhere you go? Just as that thought crossed my mind, a line of drool came floating down from the creature's mouth.

Luckily, right then, Kathy came bustling in. She dropped her things on the chair next to me as I averted my gaze from the slobber.

"Sorry I'm late. Work crisis," Kathy said, somewhat out of breath.

"Electrodes not working in the Barcalounger again?"

Kathy rolled her eyes. "We only did that once, Maggie. Once. Years ago. And no, counseling another teary co-ed," she called as she rushed over to the counter and put in her order.

"What manipulation will you be using with this one?" I asked as Kathy returned to the table.

"Ammunition in the battlefield of love, I think you mean. Besides, you made it clear in your completely misrepresented book what you thought of the enterprise," she said, pointing to my book on the table near us.

"I never mentioned the War Council by name. It was an academic discussion of dyadic communication in the romantic realm."

"It was not a purely academic book. It was about the War Council, or as we are toying with calling it now, the Love Council…"

I may have snorted some latte foam at that one. Love Council. Ha. But I refrained from commenting as Kathy took a very satisfied-looking sip from her latte and sat back.

"I needed that," she said.

"So… how are Brian and the kids?" I asked, my usual conversation starter. Kathy's husband Brian was a professor in the psychology department. The two had met in college, been married forever, and now had two pre-teens at home. (Yes, pity the children of two psychologists.)

"They're fine. Brian's back on the light deprivation study, so he took another trip to Alaska. I'll need to leave soon to get Breanna to soccer practice."

"Don't let me keep you," I said, maybe a little too sharply.

"Maggie."

"Kathy."

She gave me a look. "Any more offers for an outside research study or visiting lecturer position?"

"No. Not really." Okay, that wasn't true. I had received a number of offers following the release of the book, but nothing really jumped out at me yet. I had to admit (not to her!) that they all felt kind of tedious, and okay, maybe I had been feeling a little adrift. After processing all that the War Council and my two recent loves meant to me in the book, not to mention coming to the recent and really depressing conclusion that people suck, I wasn't quite sure what my next move should be. Inertia seemed to override everything else.

As if sensing my thoughts (who knows... maybe she had implanted electrodes in my brain as part of her War Council work), Kathy dove in again. Again! "Chickening out again like you did with the offers from Paris and New York four years ago?"

Chickening out? Chickening out? Pffft. "Well, for one, I didn't chicken out. I took time to advance my career. But I will admit I'm not sure what my next move should be."

Kathy smiled and gave me THE look. I hated that look: the head tilted down, peering over the sunglasses look that said she was oh-so-better than me. *You're not better than me, Kathy. You just aren't. I mean, look at YOUR life.* From what I could see, Kathy had become so consumed with the War Council—sorry, LOOOOVE Council—that her husband and kids were an afterthought. In the most obvious of stereotypes, she was a psychologist who needed to spend a little time looking at herself.

That said, maybe she wasn't completely wrong about me.

"Okay, fine, I'm not saying that I might not be up for a new adventure," I said.

Kathy smiled at that one. "Gotta love a double negative."

Now I was the one peering over my sunglasses, which was when I noticed that she had the tag sticking up from the back of her shirt. That was going to drive me crazy. Would she notice if I poked it down for her? I let it sit untouched. As I mentioned, inertia had become my default mode.

"What I mean is 'good,'" Kathy continued.

"Good?"

"Yeah, good."

"What do you mean by that?"

"I just think a new adventure might be good for you. Hey, maybe you could join Mike and Monique in Italy now that they go every summer."

"Italy? Why Italy?" What did Kathy know?

"Didn't you take Italian?" she said.

"A year as an undergrad, but that was eons ago," I said. "Besides, they have a reason to be in Italy. I don't." (Famous last words, and yes, I later learned that Kathy had an inkling of what was about to come from Monique.)

As I started walking home, I thought about Mike and Monique. They had been a big part of my

War Council team and two of the most disparate people you could imagine. As the Cal rugby coach, Mike had the spark plug build of a former elite athlete, while Monique was a tall, willowy, and very blonde professor of women's studies in the sociology department. They actually met when I recruited them for the War Council team. They then began hooking up after one of the War Council's more dramatic escapades at a local bar (one that brought everyone involved a slap on the wrist by the university). Then, in the most bizarre twist of all, they got married. Four years later, they spent their summers in Italy because of a long-term gig Mike had coaching at an elite-level rugby camp in a town called Bonvini. Monique used her time there to write some rather illuminating papers on the town for sociology journals. More recently, she told me she'd been asked to offer lectures to some of the university-affiliated tours of the area.

Nice work if you can get it, I thought, as I walked by the cute shops that had been popping up on my block in recent years: flower shop, bookstore, bakery, bike repair. Not that I'd ever been in any of them, I realized, but they certainly improved my walk home from the university. As I climbed the stairs and unlocked the door to my apartment, I looked around at the tranquil abode I had created. I had always found such solace in that apartment. Everything I'd gone through in the past decade—including graduate school, a first all-consuming love, a heart-rending break-up, writing my dissertation, beginning work as a professor, creating the War Council, a second love created (unbeknownst to me) using War Council techniques, and then my current status as a starting-to-be-more-well-established academic and consultant—had happened in that apartment, a.k.a. my sanctuary from the less-than-organized world outside. I still loved the place but had to admit that a malaise had been growing. The same four walls that had soothed me over the past decade started looking somewhat sterile, creating an anxious feeling. While I knew that Kathy was right, and I was ready for a new adventure, what was it meant to be?

The answer soon came in the call that led me to join the UC Berkeley Alumni Association trip to Italy in July. Of course, even that process was a little messy. You see, these sorts of alumni-association travel adventures are usually scheduled at least a year in advance (versus the two-month notice I received). They also tended to be accompanied by history or classics or geography or art history or even literature professors. That way, the professor could offer "enhancement" lectures along the way. Me? While I can tell you why a group of people will never communicate well or what qualities make certain groups more suited to a particular task than others, I'm not your gal when it comes to pointing out the significance of a particular fresco. So, receiving the request to accompany the alumni association trip to Italy that summer was a surprise. Not a bad surprise but a surprise nonetheless.

Chapter Two
MONIQUE

I don't know how I got talked into it. Well, actually, I do. To begin with, I was bored. For the past four summers—ever since I got married—I have joined my husband Mike (still getting used to saying that!) in a bucolic little town in northern Italy called Bonvini. Home to a long-established rugby academy, Mike served as its head coach during the months he wasn't coaching the UC Berkeley team. Summer sports camps in Europe are how a lot of elite-level coaches (especially those in niche sports like rugby) make extra money. I hadn't been to Europe in years—not since I did my graduate work in Paris—so I came along and played the role of loving wife. Ha! Like I said, I'm still getting used to that. Husband and wife. Especially ironic for someone like me who never thought I would get married. So provincial, I always thought. Still so misogynistic in many ways. But I loved the guy to death. He asked. I said yes. We got married on top of a mountain in Lake Tahoe, and there we were.

At first, I loved my Italian summers. As a tenured sociology professor, summer school wasn't something I had to partake in anymore, and I found taking a break from the Bay Area to live in the middle of the Italian countryside rather pleasurable. I spent the first year getting to know my surroundings and taking Italian lessons from a British ex-pat who had married a local Italian woman he'd met on a train 20 years earlier. I'd call the milieu romantic, except (as I believe I have already established) I am most decidedly not of the ilk to do so.

Embracing Italy's slow-food traditions, each day I would stroll into the village to pick up some food at the fresh market. Then I would sit at the cafe on the main square and have an espresso or a spritz, depending on the time of day. I'd wear my big Sofia Loren-style hat and sunglasses and watch the inhabitants of the town. On certain days, I would also observe the tourists traipsing through to look at the birthplace and workshop of a Renaissance-era artist of some renown. Then I would make the walk back to the cottage the sports academy provided for us on the edge of town, just up a small hill from Mike's training facility and the dormitories used by the students.

On certain days, I would extend my walk and, after dropping the groceries in the kitchen, head down the hill to the athletic facility to watch Mike coaching the rugby students. Depending on the course of study offered that week, the players ranged in age from teenagers to adults and from beginners to elite-level athletes. "Course of study." Ha! I'm not sure why I used that phrase, as I'm going to admit that I still found rugby to be a rather ridiculous endeavor. All that throwing of an odd-sized ball back and forth and then pummeling each other in order to obtain it. I mean, really, what is the purpose?

But I digress. Sometimes, if I stood on the sidelines watching long enough—still in my hat and sunglasses and wearing a short summer frock (again a la Sofia Loren)—I would catch Mike's eye and give a little nod. He would get a wicked grin on his face and nod back. I would then stroll nonchalantly into the facility's equipment room while he tapped his assistant coach, Fabrizio, and said… something… Who knows what Mike told the poor kid? I was never close enough to hear. Hopefully, it was something discreet like "I need to pick up some more knee pads" and not "Excuse me while I go bang my wife." With Mike, it really could've been either one. Still, life was good, and I enjoyed my little routine.

The second summer, after noticing the locals all rode bikes, I added a bicycle to my ritual. I made it an e-bike since the town sat perched at an elevation and the surrounding countryside was quite hilly. The bike I rented for the summer had a cute little basket in the front and a bell so I could warn wayward tourists I was behind them as I tooled through the cobblestone streets on the way to the fresh market or the cafe or passed the occasional horse and rider out on the road. Cute as a button, I was. Naturally, part of me found the image a tad nauseating, but another part reveled in the role I was playing. I even wrote papers for a few sociology journals about the effects of trying on alternate manners of living and the slow-food lifestyle on the libido. To sum it up in a word: invigorating.

My third summer in Italy proved more of a challenge. I still loved my small-town slow-food rugby-equipment-room-visiting rituals and continued with the Italian lessons and even socialized with a few locals. At a certain point, though, I'd written all the papers I could think of, and Mike and I had "enjoyed each other's company" in almost every part of the rugby facility. Hell, much of the town. I was hitting 40 and looking for, I don't know, *something*. Mike and I had discussed the possibility of procreating but decided it would either happen or it wouldn't. By that point, it appeared that it wouldn't, which was fine. Much like the idea of marriage, I had never really contemplated having a child before meeting Mike, and I was quite content with my life. Really.

To pass the time, I started examining the groups of tourists a tad more closely as they ambled by me at the cafe in town. In general,

Bonvini was quiet. The boisterous sounds of the rugby players took place outside the walls that surrounded it, and the rest of the countryside was filled with farms and wineries. But the town offered two big draws for tourists: the first being that some of those wineries were considered the finest in the region, if not the country. The other was the birthplace of Paolo Luciano, a Renaissance artist of some renown whose childhood home and first workshop had been turned into a museum just off the square where I sat. Naturally, like many other Italian towns, Bonvini also featured a lovely church, an exquisite concert hall, and artisans galore, but it was Luciano who put the town on the map for tour groups visiting the region.

I noted that the tours tended to begin with the motor coaches pulling up on the southern edge of the town. The groups would then walk through an opening in what was left of the original town walls following a flag-carrying guide down the main street. The tourists all wore telltale earpieces attached via lanyards to radios, through which they could listen to the guide discussing points of interest along the way. The radios allowed the groups—which ranged from a handful to a few dozen people—to not have to stay too close to the guide to hear the commentary. And, thankfully, for those of us enjoying our morning cappuccino, the guide did not have to shout. I noted that while some of the tourists appeared enthralled with the spiel and remained in close proximity to the guide, others took the opportunity to stop to take pictures or loiter about in a less captivated manner.

The flags these guides carried tended to be plain red or white or green (or all three to represent the Italian flag). Others denoted the names of the bigger travel operators. Occasionally, I noticed a tour guide carrying a flag affiliated with a university. Interesting. I guess I had been somewhat aware that collegiate alumni association trips existed, but they hadn't really come across my radar during my time at the university. It wasn't hard to figure out which groups were university-aligned as, in addition to the flags carried by the leader, members of the group wore caps or t-shirts emblazoned with the name of the college as they passed.

I gleaned through experience that the tours typically came through town around 10 a.m., so I started stationing myself at the outdoor table at the cafe that gave me the best view. There, I began analyzing the dynamics of the various players. In addition to the aforementioned tour guides—some I recognized as locals, others reading off a prepared text—carrying the flag in front with the group following obediently behind, I noticed what I assumed to be the tour director for the overall trip. The tour directors typically stationed themselves in the back, offering instructions to the bus driver and then madly typing into or talking on their phone. From the words I could make out in Italian or English or other languages representing the group's origin, they were making arrangements for the next stop. These tour directors ran the gamut—from young, eager, tech-savvy types taking videos of the group on their phones, to older, worn-out sorts barely going through the motions.

One day in July, I was pleasantly surprised to see what appeared to be a tour group from UC Berkeley. Many of them had donned dark blue Cal-emblazoned caps that I surmised had been provided to foster a sense of camaraderie. Others wore similarly emblazoned t-shirts and jackets. I was even more surprised to spot among the group a person who appeared to be Professor Wilcox. Intriguing. I didn't know Professor Wilcox well. We taught in different departments (me sociology and him art history) and are decades apart in age (me, as I mentioned, 40, him I presumed well into his 80s). I hadn't seen him in years but had attended a few of his lectures years earlier when working on a piece examining the symbolism of the female form in art and popular culture. It then dawned on me that as part of one of those lectures, Wilcox had mentioned his expertise when it came to the paintings and life of Paolo Luciano, the artist who hailed from Bonvini. I suppose, then, that it should not have been a complete shock to find him visiting the town. Still, I had somehow never registered the fact that professors were involved in these university-affiliated trips.

♡ *The Italy Affair* ♡

As the group drew closer, I attempted to make eye contact with Professor Wilcox, who still wore the same tweed-style jackets but otherwise appeared much more stooped and aged than I remembered. As Wilcox walked by, he happened to look in my direction, so I gave a little nod and said, *"Professore"* with a smile. He gave a little start, and I could see the gears twisting in his head as he attempted to place me outside of the usual context of the UC Berkeley campus.

"Professor DeVellier?" Professor Wilcox finally said, stopping at my table.

"In the flesh," I said, nodding.

"But what… what are you doing here?"

"This is where I spend my summers ever since Coach Banks and I got married."

Wilcox got a quizzical look on his face that made it apparent he had no idea who or what I was talking about.

"Michael Banks, Cal's rugby coach. We married four years ago."

"Ah. I will admit my knowledge of the sport of rugby is minimal."

"So was mine," I said, laughing. "Still is, I have to admit, but so is Mike's understanding of feminist sociological theory. Would you like to sit down?"

Professor Wilcox motioned to the local guide that she could continue with the tour while he took a seat at my table.

"I've taken this tour dozens of times, and they don't really need me," he said, ordering an espresso from the server, Bruno, in excellent Italian. I suppose that was to be expected from a man who had spent his career studying Italian artists. I thanked Bruno in my not-so-excellent Italian and mentioned I had seen his lovely wife and daughter at the fresh market earlier. As I had learned, part of the etiquette involved in living in a small town was the requisite small talk. (Yes, I included that in my previous year's paper.) Then I turned back to Professor Wilcox.

"I'm surprised to see you here as part of a tourist cohort," I said.

"Oh, I've been participating in these for years. Are you not familiar with the university's alumni association trips?"

"I have to admit I only recently became aware of them," I said honestly.

"Well, you should be. They are quite entertaining and a wonderful perquisite for us professors. The alumni association partners with travel operators to provide tours all over the world. On some—not all, but when they can—they send a professor along as an enrichment lecturer. It adds a bit of cachet to have an expert in the field offering lectures or insights along the way."

I laughed. "Not something they offer to us very often in sociology, but I can see you would be an ideal candidate for this one with your knowledge of Renaissance art."

He smiled, but I noted it was a bit rueful. "It has been a most enjoyable benefit to my position."

"Has been?"

Wilcox sighed. "This is the first excursion I've taken in quite a few years. It's… well… it's the first I've taken since my wife died."

I realized I had read something in a faculty communique about his wife passing away the previous year after a long battle with cancer.

"My deepest condolences," I said.

"I appreciate that. It has been somewhat difficult being back here seeing all of these precious monuments we so loved without her by my side, but I have found that it helps to keep moving."

Poor man. I made a mental note to let Mike know just how much I loved him when he had his next day off from the rugby clinics. It might even require a quick ride on the bike down to the equipment room after my talk with Professor Wilcox.

"I hope the trip is aiding in the processing of your grief," I said, patting his arm compassionately.

Wilson looked at me with a wry smile. Then the quizzical look on his face returned and he asked: "How many years did you say you have been spending your summers here?"

"This is my third."

"I noticed your proficiency with the language."

"I appreciate that. I wouldn't call it proficient, but I have been improving."

"You know…" Wilcox began, "sometimes on these trips, as part of the enrichment, the travel organizations ask locals or ex-pats to come to the hotel and elucidate on the area's customs, rituals, quirks, and the like. The travelers love hearing what it's like to actually live in Italy. You might be an ideal candidate for that sort of oratory."

"Oh?"

"Well, you have obviously learned the customs of this village quite well," Wilcox said, pointing to my seat at the cafe.

I smiled. "Again, I appreciate that. I am still learning, but I did write some papers on the rhythms of this village for a few sociology journals."

"I'll have to look them up."

"Speaking of which, I notice all of the groups arrive by bus. Where are you based?" I asked.

"They have ensconced us at a hotel in Lacusara. As you know, it's only about 30 minutes away at the base of the lake and a good headquarters hotel from which to take day trips to the smaller villages found in the countryside," Wilcox gestured to where we were sitting, "or along the lake or even into Turin or Milan, which are not far away by train. It's quite a charming hotel that specializes in tour groups."

"Interesting," I said, mentally adding the information to the notes I'd already been taking on group travel rituals.

Wilcox then pointed to the young (and very pregnant) tour director, who was now yelling into her phone quite emphatically in Italian—fast enough that I had trouble catching what she was saying.

"As it happens," he said, "the local Gabriella had lined up to give the talk to this group tomorrow evening just canceled. Would you like me to speak to her about you filling in?"

I thought about it for a second or two before answering, "I would be honored."

And that's how I began offering lectures on what I had learned about the Italian culture in Bonvini to the groups staying at the Hotel Botanico in Lacusara. As Wilcox had mentioned, the city was a 30-minute drive away on very winding roads, and my lectures were in the evening, so the groups were kind enough to put me up at the hotel for the night. I found it to be a quite civilized little hotel. Not five star, but a solid four (three-and-a-half, if you were really picky) and filled with interesting people from all over the world. It also gave me a chance to explore another Italian city, this one at the foot of a lake versus on a hilltop like Bonvini.

I quickly threw together a lecture on the cultural traditions found in a small town in the Italian countryside. Data from my papers interspersed with more light-hearted cocktail-party-style material. I mean, obviously I wasn't a local, but as an outsider, I could speak to the curiosities of Italian life as they compared to those in the States and offer a small history of the Slow Food Movement emanating from the region. My first lecture went quite well, and I even received a few laughs. As their attire had indicated, the group I found Professor Wilcox accompanying was filled with members of the UC Berkeley Alumni Association or somehow related to one or knew one. Most were hitting middle age or older, my assumption being that particular demographic had the free time and savings to afford the excursions, although there were a few younger adults. I will admit I inwardly grinned every time one of them gave a little "Go Cal" during my lecture, as the phrase served as a double entendre for Mike and me. (If you must know, when we first became intimate during our time with the War Council, the phrase served as Mike's coital exclamation.) In general, the lecture provided an enjoyable outlet and helped relieve the ennui I had been experiencing.

    Soon, word got around from that particular tour director to her tour operator and on to other tour operators, and I spent the rest of that summer giving similar lectures to other university-affiliated groups, which were more inclined to add these sorts of educational components to the tours. I surmised that my addresses proved popular because people were eager to hear about the real Italy, the one beyond the superficial traipsing through museums and churches and archeological sites. The lectures became popular enough that by the end of the summer, one tour operator even offered me a small stipend and put me up at the Hotel Botanico for their whole four-day trip so I could offer insights along the way. I learned that a majority of the groups touring the region utilized that particular hotel, which routinely hosted two to three tours at a time. As Professor Wilcox had mentioned, Hotel Botanico was designed for groups, and they all had similar itineraries, so the staff had it down to a science. Soon, so did I. I just had to learn which university to mention when I gave my talk. Overall, it was a rather agreeable assignment and gave me something to do while Mike dealt with the testosterone-filled players of all ages and genders (if you've seen a rugby scrum, you know that testosterone abounds for all) who came for the camps, even if it caused me to miss some trips to the equipment room.

Back at UC Berkeley the following winter, a few months before I left for my fourth summer in Italy (the year Maggie joined us), I received a message that the director of the alumni association travel program, Beverly Santiago, would like to meet with me. I will admit to a slight trepidation as the organization had recently changed travel directors, and I had no idea what to expect. Luckily, Beverly, a formidable woman about my height who had a slight Caribbean tint to her accent, immediately put me at ease.

"I was looking at the feedback from last year's Italy trip, and it indicated the participants loved your lecture," she said.

"I'm delighted to hear that," I said. "I was pleased when Professor Wilcox suggested it."

"I heard that you joined other groups for their whole trip," she said.

"Just one at the end of the summer."

"Would you be amenable to doing that with the group we have visiting the area this July?"

"I…"

"Before you answer, I should tell you that it's going to be a little different than the trip we offered last year."

"Oh? In what way?"

"We've added a few extra days based on feedback indicating the alumni would like a trip that immerses them more in Italian culture. The extra time will provide the opportunity to add optional activities such as language lessons or wine tasting or art classes."

"That sounds wonderful," I said. "There is definitely more to experience than is possible on the shorter trips that just hit the sights."

"Of course. Now, as you know, Professor Wilcox will again accompany the trip. He is one of the leading experts on the artist from the region, Paolo Luciano…"

"A wonderful resource," I added.

"Yes. Indeed. However, I am cognizant of the fact that he is also slowing down a little," Beverly said, "which is why I hoped you might be able to stay with them the whole time as you did for that other group."

"I don't see why not."

"I am planning to attend the trip as well."

"Oh?" I said, a little surprised.

"Yes, as the new alumni travel director, I'm still getting a handle on the current slate of trips as I begin to plan the offerings for future years. I want to see how this trip plays out on the ground, especially since it's been opened up," she said. "This will also give me a chance to assess the contracted tour operator, Scholarly Travel Adventures. That sort of thing. Don't worry. I won't interfere with what you do. I'll just be there as a guest taking it all in."

"Sounds wonderful," I said and meant it. It would be nice to have someone like Beverly along. "I'm looking forward to your participation and would be happy to advance whatever feedback I can on how the trip compares, not just to the last Cal trip, but to others I have seen or participated in."

Beverly smiled. "Excellent, just excellent."

♡ ♥ ♡

Unfortunately, a few weeks after Mike and I arrived in Italy in late May, I received an email letting me know that Beverly Santiago had broken her femur (ouch!) while on the university's trip to Egypt. Not long after that, she called and said her rehabilitation would take some time, and she would not be able to make the trip after all. Since her flights and room were already booked and paid for by the university—and she was still interested in feedback on the trip—she asked if I knew anyone adept at analysis who might take her place. It occurred to me that I did know someone: Maggie. Not only was Maggie affiliated with the university as an associate professor, but also her organizational communications expertise made her the ideal candidate to survey the trip and gauge the reaction of the participants. If I'm honest, I also thought it might be nice to have a friend along and (a tad less selfishly) something Maggie would enjoy. Although she had received a great deal of acclaim and contract business from the book she wrote on the War Council venture that brought Mike and me together, when I left her in May, I had gotten the feeling she was at loose ends.

So, at Beverly's suggestion, I made the call…

Chapter Three
EMILIO

The people, they came through the hotel where I worked as a bartender every day. *Ogni giorno*. Once the tourism season got underway in earnest each spring, we saw a new batch each week at Hotel Botanico, sometimes every few days depending on the type of tour. Some attempted to see all of Italy or even all of Western Europe in a short amount of time. Those I called the "If this is Tuesday, this must be Belgium" tours. Others explored the region in more depth. What they all had in common was the fact that their schedules were totally regimented. Breakfast buffet starting at 7 a.m., load the bus at 8:30, see the sights, return. Rinse and repeat.

The hotel hosted groups from all over the world. They came from as close as France, Germany, and Great Britain to as far as China, Japan, and Korea. Then there were the Americans. Now, I don't like to generalize... Ah, who am I kidding? I love to generalize. Don't we all? Stereotypes exist for a reason, do they not? That is not to say there are no exceptions. There are, of course, people with most decidedly non-conventional aspects to their personalities. There are just a lot more that fit a certain category. The truth is, I never really got to know most of the people who visited the hotel well enough to find much out beyond the surface. Or I didn't until that fateful group that, well, stayed a little longer.

It was one of the groups that had booked Professoressa Monique as the local contributor for the lectures that played a part in some of the rinse-and-repeat schedules. In addition to experts on topics such as history, art, and archeology, tour operators would book locals or ex-pats who lived in Italy for at least part of the year to speak on some of the wonderful inconsistencies of Italian life. Monique had become a favorite. Even for me. I really enjoyed it when Monique and her husband Mike visited the hotel, and not just because I'm half American (on my mother's side), grew up in the States, and have dual citizenship. They were also closer to my about-to-hit-40 age than the majority of the people who came through our doors. Plus, they were fun, which was not an adjective I used very often.

The previous summer, Monique had begun lecturing to some of the tour groups that made their way through the hotel. It started with a group from the college where she taught during the school year: University of California, Berkeley. After a while, other tour directors caught on to just how entertaining she could be when discussing all she had learned living in Italy the past few summers and kept asking her back. As a college professor, Monique was a natural at holding people's attention. Plus, she offered quite the dichotomy: Tall and quite striking, she came off like one of those cold, steely blondes you might find in a 1940s film noir or an Alfred Hitchcock movie. And yet she had chosen Mike, a man for whom the American slang "dude" truly fit, as her spouse. On the stockier side—in amazing shape but sturdily built—Mike coached rugby out at the sports academy in the nearby town of Bonvini. When Monique and Mike stood together, their physical presence and banter reminded me of Hepburn and Tracy or Colbert and Gable or Stanwyck and Cooper, especially in *Ball of Fire* (one of my favorite films). Like those film duos, their sexual chemistry was off the charts. You could almost feel the pheromones wafting off their bodies as they made their way through the lobby and up to my bar for a drink during the receptions the hotel held for the tour groups. I noticed that at each of the receptions, they at some point would peel off for points unknown, only to return with big grins, flushed cheeks, and rumpled clothing. It always brought a smile to my face. *Sempre, sempre, sempre.* Good for them.

With some groups, Monique stayed at the hotel. Mike would come with her to the opening reception and then head back to the Bonvini Rugby Academy. Because of this, I got to know Monique better than Mike, which was too bad. I'm not saying she wasn't lovely. Not at all. It's just that, from what I could see, Mike was most amusing, and I would have enjoyed getting to know him better.

The truth is, although I had been living in Lacusara for a half dozen years, I did not have many friends. The locals tended to be entrenched in their own lives, and most people my age were married and had families. It was also a bit by design. After leaving my graduate program in Florence following the collapse of my marriage, I had kind of kept to myself. Honestly, my opinion of the human race had fallen quite a bit. Years spent serving people drinks in a hotel after having your heart broken will do that for you. So, when I wasn't working, I tended to enjoy my solitude.

Although my schedule varied, most days followed a similar symmetry: I would get up early and walk across town and through the botanical garden to the Hotel Botanico (named, as you may have guessed, for its proximity to the garden). There, I would make a slew of coffee drinks and prepare the bar for later that evening. During my four-hour break between shifts, I would retreat to my small apartment, again using the route that took me through the botanical garden. Sometimes I would linger on one of the benches. The garden had become my favorite place in the city, filled as it was with an assortment of flowers, trees, lily ponds, and sculptures—plus, of course, many of the town's citizens. I would see students peering over their laptops, young couples strolling, and older residents sitting on the benches.

Groups of tourists also made their way through the garden each day. I often looked for the telltale flags the guides carried and then headed in the opposite direction or hid behind one of the trees. It's not that I had any opposition to running into guests from the hotel. Let's just say that there were a few local guides of the female persuasion I preferred to avoid due to my own stupidity. When I first moved to Lacusara, I made the mistake of thinking it would help heal my broken heart to enter into a few dalliances I thought to be casual, only to be proven completely and totally wrong. I had recently decided, yet again, that it might be in my best interest to stay away from all people, especially those of the female persuasion, beyond my very superficial encounters at the hotel. I just really didn't have a lot of luck with the species, it would seem.

I wasn't feeling a lot of luck in life at all. After the demise of my life in Florence, I did not want to return home to Brooklyn in disgrace. By moving to Lacusara, I could live as a stranger (regrettable dalliances aside). I was the anonymous bartender who served the coffee drinks in the morning and the cocktails in the evening and spent his days walking from his apartment to the hotel and back through the botanical garden. Yes, I realize my routine held a similar rinse and repeat to the one I judged the tour groups on. At least they were doing it in a new location. Seeing the world. Not me.

That's why I so enjoyed the company of Mike and Monique. When they started coming to the hotel, they brought a liveliness to the proceedings. When I saw them for the first time that year—the year everything changed—it was late May. They sidled up to the bar and stayed to chat with me as I handed my 8,000th Aperol Spritz into expectant hands. (I may be embellishing that a little bit, but I made a ridiculous number of the drinks on a daily basis.)

"*Salve*, Mike."

"*Ciao,* Emilio. How's it shaking?"

"It is still … shaking," I said. That's bartender talk, in case you are not fluent.

"Good to hear."

"*Buona sera,* Emilio," Monique said, always more formal than her husband.

"*Buona sera, Professoressa*. What may I make for you?" I asked.

Monique nodded toward the spritz while Mike said he would have a Peroni beer. Luckily, I had put extras on ice as we had a group from Australia in-house, and they tended to go through beers faster than groups from other countries.

"Has the rugby academy opened for the season?" I asked Mike.

"Next week. I've been working with the staff and making sure the equipment room is all set up," Mike said, glancing in Monique's direction and smiling.

"Michael!" Monique said, hitting his shoulder while also smiling. "How about you, Emilio? Has the season started in earnest for the hotel?"

"For a while now. We started seeing more groups in April," I said. "The spring tours tend to be the shorter ones, only staying for two to three days or so, so the groups have been in and out."

"A lot of .'*Benvenuta in l'Italia*!' and then '*Arrivederci*,' eh?" Mike said.

When he said, "*Benvenuta in l'Italia*," Mike looked at Monique with another grin. She slapped him on the shoulder again while looking over toward the elevators at a room the hotel used to store luggage. Not sure what that was about.

"Is your university coming back this summer?" I asked.

Monique broke out of her brief reverie, turned back to me, and nodded. "Yes. In July. Actually, that particular trip should prove interesting as they added a few days to their normal tour as a way to offer what they're calling a 'more immersive' travel experience."

"That does sound interesting," I said, not knowing just how interesting it would all turn out to be.

Chapter Four
MAGGIE

Once I agreed to the Italy trip—first by giving a tentative okay to Monique and then confirming my participation with Cal's Alumni Association travel director, Beverly Santiago (broken femur? The poor thing!)—the onslaught of information began. First, I received the full itinerary. I noted thankfully that we were staying at the same hotel for the whole trip, a place called Hotel Botanico in a lakeside town called Lacusara. We would then be taking day trips that included boat rides on the lake, tours of nearby archeological sites, and visits to some of the smaller towns and well-known wineries in the area. Perfect. I'm personally not a fan of trips that have you move hotels every night. I took a few of those with my parents as a child, and they were horrifying. Thank god, at first glance, the schedule for this one looked very civilized.

Then I received a large box from the tour operator, an outfit called Scholarly Travel Adventures, filled with what can best be described as travel-related knickknacks. I pulled out a cloth backpack and water bottle emblazoned with their logo. A tad tacky but fine. I then found name badges. Ugh. What were we in, kindergarten? Or worse, at a convention? Or even worse, a team-building event? I also discovered a small plastic box with a bunch of plugs—ah yes, power converter. Nice. Made me realize I should check my passport. I happily discovered it was still up to date and remembered I had renewed it when I thought I might join Nick in Paris. I felt a little pang as I looked at the passport, not only because of Nick but because I had also updated my passport all those years ago when I thought I would go with Bill to Tokyo. Before he broke my heart, which caused me to create the War Council and then meet Nick and…

Stop it, Maggie, I thought. *Stop questioning. You made the right decision then, and you're making the right decision now.*

I then found a list of the alumni attending the trip, along with their pictures and bios. I flipped through the batch and could already formulate a few personality archetypes based on the photos they chose and how much of a bio they had included. The lawyer, doctor, and scientist types pretty much just listed their CVs while others took more creative routes (favorite trips, hobbies, etc.). Then there was one with nothing. Just a name: Clark Johnson. *Whatcha hiding there, Clark?* I laughed and reminded myself to

♡ Maggie ♡

be open-minded. I was not analyzing the group, only providing feedback on the trip itself. That's when I saw the professor accompanying the trip: Professor Wilcox? That cranky old bastard? I'd only encountered the man a few times at faculty mixers, but to say I found him to be a pompous bore would be sugarcoating it. *Oh, this will be so fun,* Monique had said.

I picked up my phone, noting the time: 9 a.m. in Berkeley so around 6 p.m. in Italy. When Monique answered, I didn't even say hello. "Did you know Wilcox was the professor on this trip?"

Silence. Then, "Maybe."

"Yikes, Monique. You heard me. Yikes."

"In my defense, I saw him here in Italy last year, and he's just been so sad since his wife died. It's like all the life has been drained out of him. I didn't want to have to handle him on my own again."

I laughed. "Not much of a defense."

"For me it is!" she said, laughing as well. "I know, I know. We'll still have fun. You'll see. Besides, Wilcox is ancient, and he does his own thing. So can we." Monique paused for a bit. "He'll be surrounded by his groupies anyway."

"Groupies?" I tried to picture the elderly art history professor with whom I had such trouble creating small talk having groupies.

"Wilcox is a font of information when it comes to Renaissance art, especially as it relates to the famous artist from the area, Paolo Luciano, although I think he's fallen out of favor a bit—Luciano, not Wilcox. Wilcox is just old. And sad. But some of the alumni who take these trips just love him. They either had him as a professor, saw him lecture, or traveled somewhere else with him. To them, he's a celebrity. You'll see. It's rather humorous. They jostle to stand next to him during the tours or invite him to dinner on the free nights. You know, groupies."

I laughed again. "Okay. I'll take your word for it."

"Don't worry. I'm sure they're going to love you, too."

"Oh god, I hope not. You promised me I could just be a bemused bystander and offer a report of what I see." *I mean, I'm not going to have to participate in anything, am I?*

"That's somewhat true, but also something you might find to be a bit impossible."

"Ugh. You know I hate groups."

Now Monique laughed. "But you study groups!"

"Which is why I absolutely hate them and, well, people."

"Well, you like Mike and me, I hope."

"You know I do."

"And I can promise you will love the setting."

"I'm going to hold you to that, you know."

"I can't wait to see you, my friend."

"Same here."

I hung up the phone and realized I really was looking forward to seeing Monique and Mike—definite exceptions to my "people suck" axiom.

♡ Maggie ♡

♡ ♥ ♡

Now Kathy is still a work in progress, I thought, four weeks later when we got together for our usual latte the day before I was scheduled to depart for Italy. And, yes, I realized how snarky that sounded even in my head. Then she went and ruined the snark.

"I'm going to miss you, you know," Kathy said, taking a sip from her latte.

I looked at her. She barely seemed to tolerate me. Why in the hell would she miss me?

"You okay?" I asked.

"Fine," she said a little too quickly. "Why do you ask?"

"Just wondering… You seem a little out of sorts," I said, looking at her shirt, which had one of the bottom buttons twisted backward. What was that all about?

"Well, I'm fine." Now *that* was a definite snap.

"Okay…"

Kathy looked at me as if suddenly recognizing my presence. "Sorry. Maybe I have been a little out of sorts lately. This Love Council…"

"War Council," I muttered under my breath, and she gave me a stern look.

"…Love Council business has gotten a little overwhelming. My assistant and two coordinators quit—well, they graduated and got 'real jobs.'" Yes, she used air quotes. "So we are a little understaffed at the moment. And with Brian still in Alaska…"

"Wait, I thought he was coming back once we passed the solstice, which was, what, a few weeks ago?"

"So did I," she sighed. "So did I. He said it will just be another couple of days."

"Sorry to miss his return."

"No, you're not."

I laughed. I will admit I did find Brian to be a little on the dull side. "No, probably not. But I am hoping he comes back soon for your sake."

"Thanks," she said, looking at me with an almost rueful expression. "I appreciate that." I got a smile. "And you."

Okay, now I really knew something was up, but by then, she was already packing up to go. Last one to arrive, first to leave.

"Are you sure you're okay?"

"I'm fine," she snapped. Okay, back to the snippiness.

"See you when I get back, then?"

"Count on it," Kathy said, starting to rush off. She got a few steps before stopping and turning. "Have fun. You know. For me."

Now that was definitely weird, but I just nodded and said, "I will."

I went back to my apartment to complete the last-minute packing ahead of my flight the following morning. With so many things to remember, there was a huge part of me that at that moment would have preferred staying home. But, no, I reminded myself, an adventure would be good for me. I needed this. Still, what a pain in the butt travel prep can be!

The following morning, I picked up a ride share in front of the flower shop downstairs and took it to the nearest BART station. I rode the train to San Francisco International Airport with my fingers crossed that the flight would be leaving on time. San Francisco's notorious fog meant more delays than most airports, to the point where I had this theory that they threw a huge margarita party the one day a year when all the flights departed on time. As I made my way through security, I encountered a series of what can only be described as "cluster fucks" that put my organizational impulses on high alert. With security rules changing so frequently, no one knew exactly what to do. Shoes on or off? Electronics in the case or out? How many ounces for fluids? In or out of the bag? Luckily, I had applied for Global Entry at the same time I renewed my passport and breezed through the TSA Precheck line without having to remove my shoes or my laptop or any other indignities. After dodging inattentive people left and right—*Sure, ma'am, why not just stop right in the middle of the passageway to send a text? The 20 of us walking behind you don't mind stopping*—I made it to the waiting area for the flight with a good 45 minutes to spare. I made a note to add a chapter to my "people suck" book on the lengths to which they really suck in airports.

Once I reached the waiting area, I took a deep breath and scanned the crowd to see if I could identify anyone from the materials packet I had received. I didn't need to look far to recognize a few as they were already wearing their name tags. Really? At the airport?

Then, I felt a curmudgeonly presence on my left. "Professor McGrew."

"Professor Wilcox," I said, turning in his direction and nodding. Monique's description of him proved apt. He definitely appeared a lot older and sadder than I remembered. Same tweed jacket though.

"I will admit to a bit of surprise when I saw your name attached to this trip," Wilcox said.

"Did you now?"

"You do realize I will be the one offering the lectures," he said. "The region's art is my area of specialty."

"Duly recognized," I said. "I am only on the trip to observe and report back to the travel office on the logistics. I have no desire to speak or engage at all in the proceedings. But do know that I am happy to offer any academic or moral support you may require."

Wilcox blinked about five times, trying to decide (I assumed) just how sincere I was being. Truth be told, I wasn't sure myself. I didn't really know the man except by reputation and my few encounters with him. Although communication studies and art history were both part of the broader School of Letters & Sciences, communication studies fell under social sciences while art history fell under arts & humanities. This meant that our paths almost never crossed except in the occasional giant lecture hall or mixer in the faculty lounge. Until now. Still, Monique had told me about the loss of his wife a year and a half earlier—and her long illness before that—and the man definitely had a palpable sadness encircling him. I didn't know him well enough to mention that I knew about his wife, so I just nodded sympathetically.

Wilcox nodded back. Then we noticed a pack of about a half dozen of the older alumni (the ones wearing their name badges, naturally) walking slowly in our direction. It had a bit of a Night of the Living Dead quality to it, so I backed off and took in the rest of the waiting crowd as they made their way toward Wilcox. While some in the travel group were flying with us from San Francisco, others would be coming from other airports or had flown in a little early and would meet us in Italy. In addition to the badge groupies (as I now called them), based on the pictures I'd seen I was able to pick out a cute older couple in the distance sitting quietly together holding hands, plus a few younger people—by younger I mean 50s or late 40s, not young young—and one that was young young (20s) standing beside what I'm assuming were her parents or other relatives. I also spotted a scowling man standing next to a pillar and staring at the Cal crowd. I wondered if it might be the mysterious no-picture, no-bio Clark. Definite red flag on him, if so.

"Professor Wilcox, so nice to see you again," I heard a woman I guessed to be in her late 70s say next to me. "Paul and I are so looking forward to traveling with you again."

"And I you, Lillian. And I you," Wilcox said, cheering up just a bit. I could see that he was capable of charm and that this kind of diversion definitely benefited him. Interesting.

"In case you haven't met her, this is another UC Berkeley professor who will be traveling with us," Wilcox continued, pointing to me, even though I had added a little separation between us. That gained him a few brownie points, I have to admit. "Professor Maggie McGrew from the communications department."

There was a brief moment of interest from the group.

"Professor McGrew specializes in organizational communication."

And then it was gone. When people heard "communications," they usually assumed I studied mass communications—you know, TV, film, glitzy stuff—not group dynamics.

"Your familiarity with my work surprises me," I said to Wilcox as the first boarding announcements came from the gate attendants, and people splintered off to get their bags and make sure their documents were all in order.

"Oh, indeed. I was particularly taken with your most recent tome," Wilcox said.

He read the War Council book? Interesting.

"I didn't think it fell into the realm of the fine art you usually study, Professor Wilcox."

"Perhaps not my usual mode of academic discourse, but I knew it ruffled a few feathers—including our dean's..." He chuckled, and I remembered it was the art history department's dean whose kerfuffle sent the War Council off campus. "I admired your dissection of the theories at play," he continued.

"Thank you. I appreciate that," I said, realizing I had never read or even contemplated reading any of his books or papers. "I look forward to your lectures on the trip."

Wilcox got a smug smile that said he knew he was good at what he did. That intrigued me. Maybe it wouldn't be so bad traveling with him after all. Soon, we heard the boarding call, and everybody began the slow shuffle onto the plane. The flight itself was uneventful—if you count being crammed into a small seat in a metal cylinder for 12 hours as uneventful. *What, they can't send the professors business class?* I thought. I mean, I knew I should be grateful for the free trip and all, but the sight of those lie-flat seats in the front made my mouth water as I wound myself into a little pretzel in economy, pressing my head against the window for leverage.

After catching up on some movies and getting a fitful amount of sleep followed by a breakfast that's not worth describing, I heard the wheels hit the tarmac and then the "ding" that meant the seatbelt sign had been turned off and we could depart. I peeled myself out of my seat and attempted to look semi-presentable as the passengers started the slow move back out of the plane. We shuffled through customs and immigration, and then through frosted glass doors into the main part of the terminal. There, I started looking for the guide we were told would be greeting us at the airport.

Organizational whiz that I am, I had managed to get everything I needed into two carry-on bags. (Yes, my "personal item" was on the large size.) This made me the first one of the group to make it through the sliding doors and into the main lobby. I found a woman wearing a collared shirt with a small "Scholarly Travel Adventures" logo on the top left corner holding a sign that said "UC Berkeley Northern Italy." She'd written the word "Immersion" at the end, somewhat sloppily, if you ask me—almost as if the word was mocking us. Interesting start.

Hitting what appeared to be late middle age, the woman had short gray hair and a serious furrow in her brow as she scanned the passengers exiting through the frosted doors. I gave my best wave in her direction and saw an immediate sigh of relief.

"Oh, thank god," she said in an accent I couldn't immediately place but sure didn't sound Italian. "I was hoping they didn't send you all out the wrong exit."

"Only one exit that I saw. The others are right behind me," I said helpfully. The woman looked me up and down as if appraising my ability to be helpful at all. "I'm Maggie McGrew, one of the professors on the trip."

She rolled her eyes as if *knowing* I was not going to be any help at all.

"I'm Hilda from Scholarly Travel Adventures," she said. "I'm the tour director for this trip. I do hope you plan to be on time for the scheduled activities."

Wow. And a how-do-you-do-to-you-too— although I have to say I appreciated her desire to keep things organized. "You can bet on it," I said with what I hoped was a sincere smile.

"Uh-huh." She didn't sound sure. "Stand there," she said, pointing to a pole about 20 feet away.

"Okay…" I said, eyeing an espresso counter close by. "Although I might just grab…"

"No grabbing. Stand. Stand there," Hilda barked.

"Uh, okay. Even though, really, some of them might take a while and it's right…"

"What did I say?"

Suddenly, I felt like I was in third grade. What the hell? My brain still addled from the plane ride, I dutifully stood on my mark next to the pole instead of arguing with her. In about 30 minutes (plenty of time to grab an espresso!), Hilda finally had the rest of our crew corralled. I counted about 15. I knew the group ultimately totaled closer to 25, but some were taking other flights or had come to Europe early and would be making their way to our hotel by train or bus or car or whatever other transportation options might exist. Those of us on this flight traipsed onto a waiting bus. I took a seat by myself and felt relieved when no one joined me. As I learned in my short conversation with our Cruella de Ville tour director, I was not capable of small talk at this point in the day, and all I could think about after almost 20 hours of travel door-to-door was that I wanted a shower as soon as possible.

I slipped off the bus and into the hotel and grabbed a key card with my name on it from a hotel clerk. I was so exhausted and jet-lagged that if you later asked me to pull that person out of a line-up, I would not have been capable of it. As I headed up to my room, I promised myself I would be more social at the reception later that night, although that promise waned with each passing step as I made my way down the longest hall in history to my door at the very end. *Really? The last door?* I slipped my key card in and entered.

The room was … adequate. Perfectly clean and well-organized (yay!), but lacking in anything that might be considered luxury amenities. Totally fine. All I really wanted was clean. I was happy to find a row of hooks on the wall. If there was one thing I had learned from traveling to hotels on my book tour, it's that hooks were invaluable and something few seem to realize. Jackets, hats, bags, everything can go on a hook.

It just makes traveling so much easier. I made a mental note to mention that in my report to the university travel office. Not that the report would most likely ever make it back to the hotel itself. Maybe I could work it into a book. Unfortunately, "the role of hooks in hotel rooms as an aid in communication when people suck" probably wasn't going to cut it.

Now, the bathroom proved interesting. It had the requisite bidet we Americans find so exotic, and the shower was the smallest thing I'd ever seen. For the second time in 24 hours, I appreciated the fact I still went to yoga three times a week and wondered how Monique, amazon that she was, handled the Italian showers. Not only was it small, but it had a nozzle atop a rod that kept slipping downward, so I had the interesting sensation of trying to crouch lower and lower to get the shampoo rinsed out of my hair. Try that while jet-lagged and sleep-deprived.

As I dressed, I peeked out the window and noticed I had a pretty decent view of what appeared to be the town square. It had a fountain in the middle, cafes on every corner, and a park lining one side. Cute. Adorable, even. It was only 2 o'clock in the afternoon and although every muscle in my body (and brain) was telling me to lie down and take a nap, I knew it would be better to try to stay awake until evening to help adjust to the time change and alleviate the jet lag. I also realized I was starving, and it would be hours before our opening reception and dinner, so I decided to venture out on a walk and grab something to eat.

Once outside the hotel, I walked over to the square and found a seat at the closest cafe to the hotel, which the sign identified as "Pietro's." With my decade-old (and rudimentary at their peak) Italian skills not immediately popping into my head, I just pointed to something on the menu that looked like it might resemble pasta. When the dish arrived, it ended up being part of a lunch special that also came with a salad and a glass of wine. Okay, then. "When in Rome" (or Lacusara), as they say.

As I took a bite of the pasta (yes, amazing; no, I did not take a picture for social media as that's really not my thing), I started looking around at the cafe, the square, and the park, all framed by the lake in the distance. Beautiful, yes, but also lacking any discernible organization—or at least the sort of organization I might be familiar with. Not just throwing in salads and wine when they're not ordered (ha!), but a willy-nilly-ness to the traffic patterns that my jet-lagged brain had trouble processing.

I looked around at the other people in the cafe. There was a table with two young couples talking and laughing, the empty plates and beer bottles indicating they had been there awhile, with a yellow lab slumbering at their feet. Another table had two middle-aged men playing chess, also with dogs (a chihuahua and a German shepherd) at their feet. One of the men was wearing a collared shirt with a sweater tied around his neck that gave him the look of a character out of a Fellini movie. At another table, a very well-dressed older woman sat by herself with an equally well-coiffed dog sitting at her feet. It appeared to be a Pekinese. Hard to tell what it was under all that hair. Truth be told, it could have just been a very fluffy footstool, but then I saw the creature wiggle a little bit.

I then noticed all the people walking their dogs in the park across the way. Huh. I guess Italians love their dogs? Then I noticed something peculiar about the dogs. It was subtle at first: a young woman walking her golden retriever, a couple with a French bulldog, a tall older man with a greyhound (Italian, of course). While at first, it all seemed quite random, I suddenly noticed that every dog was a different breed, from a St. Bernard to a Jack Russell terrier. No two were alike. Why, in a town where seemingly everyone had a dog, did it seem that no one had the same breed of dog? Was there some edict that only one of each breed (and they appeared to mostly be purebred) was allowed? And, if so, who kept the ledger? I laughed a bit at the fact that these were the thoughts swimming around in my (again very jet-lagged) head and realized, *What the hell, I'm in Italy! I'm eating pasta, sipping wine, and sitting in a cafe looking out at the town square and the people walking their dogs, with a gorgeous lake backed by hills in the distance.*

I took a deep breath and turned my face to the warm sun. And then, for the first time in a long time, a smile broke out on my face—a real "it's good to be alive" smile that made all the machinations I had to go through to get me to this place worth it. Thank you, Italy. Even in all your messiness, I could tell the trip was going to be good for me. What I didn't know was just how good.

Chapter Five
MONIQUE

I spotted Maggie as she came down the stairs and into the reception area of the Hotel Botanico. I tapped Mike on the shoulder and nodded in her direction.

"Mags!" Mike shouted, a tad too boisterously in my opinion. I will admit, however, that while I found his ebullient outburst rather excessive, it also kind of ignited me as I knew what was coming next. As I mentioned previously, our trysts back in Berkeley typically culminated with Mike yelling "Go Cal!" Here in Italy, he had developed an exclamation with a more Italian flair.

"*Benvenuto in l'Italia!*" Mike continued, giving Maggie a warm hug while winking in my direction. Yep. There it was. Our new phrase: *Benvenuto in l'Italia.*

You bastard, I thought as I smiled and felt (as usual) my midsection radiating heat from the heart to points south. I looked back at Mike, at his strong chest and naturally sun-streaked hair.

He added an eyebrow raise and a wicked grin and the radiating increased. With my staying at the hotel more often while helping out on the tours, there had been fewer "visits to the equipment room." Heck, there had been weeks that it was only at these opening and closing receptions that we got a chance to see each other. To, you know, be *near* each other. Not sure what it was about this man, but even after four years of marriage (and yes, I know that's not many in the grand scheme of things), I still had the hots for him like nobody's business. And no, in case you are wondering, I do not normally speak like that *at all*. Who says "hots"? I do, in my head, when thinking about Michael Banks, that's who.

I took a couple deep breaths and managed to say, "Good to see you, Maggie," in a much more tempered tone, even as I continued to exchange glances with Mike to let him know that if the luggage closet we had discovered off the lobby happened to be available, we might want to, you know, give it a look. He nodded and tilted his head in that direction.

"Really, so so good to see you," I said, shaking off my desire for Mike and instead giving Maggie a hug.

"You, too!" Maggie said, standing back and appraising Mike and me. "Italy is good for you two, it would seem."

What an odd thing to say. Italy was just a country, a setting, after all. I remained the same person I was back in Berkeley. Besides, as I said: "Maggie, we just saw you on campus two months ago."

"And you look a lot less uptight."

Uptight? Moi? Monique DeVilliers, the professor everyone called Professor Hard Ass? I glanced at Mike and his wicked-ass smile. Okay, I suppose I was a little less edgy here in Italy where no one knew me and not back on campus where everyone had preconceived ideologies based on my position at the university. I also remembered that Maggie's superpower was her ability to size up people at a glance. She probably caught the looks between Mike and me and the flush in our cheeks. *Damn you, Maggie McGrew.* Although I knew utilizing her superpower for some heavy hitters in Silicon Valley had proven lucrative, and it was after all the reason I had invited her on this trip, I didn't like it being used on me.

"Okay, then, how about everybody else?" I said, pointing to the crowd and desperately trying to get the focus off of me.

"What about them?" Maggie asked.

"Do your thing," Mike said. "Size everyone up for us."

"I am not a show pony, Mike."

"Come on… Here, we'll get you a drink first."

Mike and I walked Maggie over to the bar, where we found Emilio holding court as usual.

"*Buona sera,* Emilio," I said.

"*Buona sera, Professoressa* Monique," Emilio said, "and Coach Mike."

"*Aperol Spritz, per favore,*" I said and held up three fingers. "*Tre.*"

"Aperol Spritz?" Maggie asked.

"That's what everybody drinks around here. You'll love it."

Emilio handed us our drinks and Maggie took a sip. A smile came over her face. "Not bad. Not bad at all."

She nodded at Emilio, who nodded back with a smile.

"*Grazie tante,* Emilio," I said.

"*Prego.*"

"Your Italian is pretty good," Maggie said.

"It's really not, but you learn a few phrases pretty quickly."

"You don't want to know some of the phrases I've learned over the years," Mike said. "The local players and coaches come up with some doozies."

"I'm sure I don't, Mike," Maggie said, laughing.

I nodded over at Emilio. "Emilio actually speaks perfect English—his mom is American and he grew up there—but I personally feel that it's more respectful to speak Italian since we are, after all, in Italy."

Maggie got a bigger smile. "We are, aren't we? I still can't believe it."

"Oh, I am so glad you came." I gave her shoulder a squeeze.

"Me, too, Monique. Thank you for thinking of me."

"Of course! So, now… do it."

"Do what?"

"Your thing," I said, pointing to the growing crowd of jet-setting UC Berkeley alumni. "I could see you analyzing Mike and me, so now let's have some fun with the other travelers, shall we? We will be spending a lot of time with them in the next week."

Maggie threw me a disappointed look and said, "I thought I was evaluating the trip, not the people," as we moved to the side of the bar.

"That's true, but why not take stock of some of the personalities as a start?"

"Fine," she said. We turned to look toward the line that had emerged at the bar as Emilio continued to hand out drinks while chatting with Mike. "My first impression is that they're all very earnest."

I nodded. "Those choosing to attend a university-aligned trip that includes educational enhancements do tend to exhibit a more earnest demeanor," I offered.

"See, you don't need me," Maggie said, smiling as we watched a couple whose husband ordered for both of them in very fractured Italian while the wife rolled her eyes. "Okay, so there you have your typical alpha coupled with a passive-aggressive."

"Noted," I said as the next man in line started describing the history of Aperol to those behind him.

"Know-it-all," we both said, laughing.

"Alas, also a common component on university-affiliated trips," I said.

We turned our attention to a man somewhat on the younger side for this group—in other words, entering middle age, not exiting it. He hovered a few steps to the side of the crowd in line for the bar, not completely getting into the line, but then sighing loudly when others moved ahead of him.

"That one might be a challenge," Maggie said.

"Really?" The man looked pretty benign to me, but what did I know? I noted his nametag, which identified him as "Clark."

"Yup."

Then, a couple who appeared to be in their mid to late 80s slowly made their way to the front of the line. They had their arms linked and shared a sweet smile as they did. In short, they were adorable.

"Life goals," Maggie said with a sigh. "I saw them at the airport. Their body language could not be sweeter."

I gave Maggie a smile and another shoulder hug. It wasn't often you found someone as special as I had with my rugby jock (more words I never thought I would utter). I looked in Mike's direction with a smile. Hopefully, Maggie would find her version of Mike. I then pointed at Emilio, laughing at something Mike said.

"How about him, then?"

Maggie smiled and gave a little shrug. "Not bad on the eyes."

I took that as a good sign that she hadn't given up on men. I then noticed Professor Wilcox waving at us from across the room.

"I believe we are being summoned," Maggie said, noticing it as well.

"That we are. Don't worry. As I said, I've worked with him before. He really is harmless. And remember, you are here to enjoy the experience and let Beverly in the alumni travel office know your thoughts. Zero responsibilities."

Those last two words I would later regret. Maggie nodded as we walked over to Wilcox.

"Time to make our introductory address," Wilcox said. "You know the drill, Professor DeVillier. I will, of course, let them know when you will be giving your talk and introduce you as well, Professor McGrew, even though you will not be offering any lectures."

"Duly noted, Professor Wilcox," said Maggie. "As I mentioned at the airport, you are the designated professor on this trip. We are just here to support you in any way we can." Maggie added a sly smile that only I picked up. She had already proven rather adept at handling him.

"Most appreciated, Professor McGrew and Professor DeVillier," Wilcox said.

"Please, Maggie."

"And Monique," I said for the umpteenth time. Every time I met the man, he did the same thing. He smiled. Maggie smiled. Smiles all around. I fought the urge to roll my eyes. Too many people watching.

"Maggie. Monique." He nodded and blinked his eyes rapidly as if digesting the information. Again. "Emory."

"Emory," we both said in unison, although I immediately realized why I'd continued calling him Wilcox.

Then Wilcox grabbed a large bag containing a few dozen "Cal" emblazoned baseball-style caps. "Would you mind handing these out?" Wilcox asked, fumbling a bit with the bag. "It's something that the travel office requests of us."

"Not at all," I said.

"I am not wearing a Cal cap," Maggie whispered as we started handing them out to the group.

"Don't worry. You won't have to," I whispered back, smiling as hands continued reaching out to snatch the caps from my grasp. *If there's anything people love, it's freebies,* I thought, although I observed a number of people who hung back and continued chatting, mentally noting them as those whose company I would no doubt prefer.

"May I have everyone's attention?" Wilcox said, turning to the group. I noticed that Hilda, the tour director from Scholarly Travel Adventures, immediately maneuvered herself to his other side. Wilcox nodded at her presence, but it was apparent he found the move to be rather presumptuous. Truthfully, so did I. From what I had observed, tour directors typically stayed in the background handling logistics while the university representatives performed the ceremonial roles. Every so often, a tour director might jockey for power with a professor, but those were usually the over-eager young ones, which this one was most decidedly not. I actually hadn't met this particular tour director before, but her body language and tone immediately suggested that she thought she knew it all and was not going to be timid about expressing that. I looked over at Maggie to see how accurate my assessment might be, but her face proved somewhat unreadable as Wilcox began speaking.

"On behalf of the university, I would like to welcome all of you to the Hotel Botanico in the beautiful lakeside town of Lacusara. We at UC Berkeley are very pleased that you have joined us for an extended version of our annual "Art Towns of Northern Italy" excursion. As you know, this trip will diverge a bit from the usual six-day trips where we had to interface with as many sights as possible in a short period of time. With the extra days, we can immerse ourselves more in the area's magnificent culture. I will, of course, still be offering evening lectures on the history of the artists from the region. We will also be joined one evening by a curator from the archaeological museum, and Professor DeVellier will offer observations on the Slow Food Movement and other local insights," he said, pointing to me, and I gave a small wave.

"We will, of course, still have the planned group excursions, which Hilda from Scholarly

Travel Adventures will facilitate," Wilcox said, pointing to Hilda, who waved emphatically as he rolled his eyes.

"Thank you, Professor Wilcox," Hilda shouted, to his obvious discomfort. "I would like to clarify that while this schedule is a little more spread out than the trips we usually facilitate at Scholarly Travel Adventures…" She turned to glare at Wilcox as if it was his decision to open up the trip. "We do still need to keep to the listed schedule."

Hilda then pointed to a bulletin board bearing UC Berkeley and Scholarly Travel Adventures logos that had been placed in the front area of the lobby adjacent to boards for the other groups staying in the hotel. "That bulletin board will be updated each evening with the most up-to-date information regarding the following day's itinerary. It's important that we stick to the listed times as otherwise I can't get you in to see the museums and ruins and other important sights in the best possible light."

"While I admire her quest for organization," Maggie whispered in my direction, "her demeanor could use some work."

"Agreed," I, well, agreed.

"Are those two always at odds?" Maggie asked.

"No. I mean, Wilcox had no trouble with the tour director last year," I said and then nodded at Hilda. "This one is new to me. I've never seen her before."

"Huh," Maggie said. Before I could ask what that meant, Hilda began shouting again.

"As you can see, tomorrow we start with a boat ride on the lake with stops at some of the towns along the way. The following day, we will take a walking tour of Lacusara that will include the botanical garden and the cathedral, followed by free time for lunch or shopping, before returning to the hotel…"

Wilcox continued to look quite agitated at the fact that Hilda had jumped in on what I surmised had been a planned elocution as to the merits of the area artists inspired by Paolo Luciano. As he attempted to regain control and she continued with her litany of the events of the next few days, I turned to look at Maggie. Her eyes scanned between them and the crowd like a laser beam seeking its target. She was taking it all in, and I hoped she would provide more of her unvarnished analysis to me (in private, of course) soon. Oh, this was enjoyable. While I loved my bucolic life each summer in Italy and my *Bienvenuto in l'Italia* trysts with Mike, I had to admit I was in dire need of a little intrigue. This particular trip could prove just the ticket. Perhaps we could even War Council Professor Wilcox and Hilda. As much as I abhorred the verbing of proper nouns, it made sense to see if our War Council protocols could help them learn to work in tandem instead of at cross-purposes.

Then I noticed Emilio, the bartender, looking over at us. More accurately, he was staring at Maggie wearing a beguiled look on his face. I looked back at Maggie, oblivious to the attention.

When Wilcox and Hilda were interrupted by the hotel's general manager announcing dinner, we all started moving into the dining room, and I realized that this could prove to be a most interesting trip.

Benvenuto in l'Italia indeed.

Chapter Six
EMILIO

Now this one was different. Maggie, they called her. Signorina Maggie. Or, okay, just Maggie. I did grow up in Brooklyn, after all. Monique and Mike, my two favorite visitors to the hotel, had brought a friend. A friend in my general age bracket. *Benissimo,* as they say. The first thing I noticed about Maggie at the opening reception for the UC Berkeley group was her striking appearance. She had long, straight black hair she kept pulled back off her face and green eyes that radiated a deep intelligence. Based on what I could overhear of her conversation with Mike and Monique, she also seemed to have some sort of special skill at sizing up people. That was unusual for the *professori* that usually accompanied these trips. First of all, many of them were older—tenured or emeritus types whose teaching load allowed them the time off and for whom these trips were a perk. And while most of them were, naturally, quite adept in providing information on art or literature or history—the topics that came in handy when visiting Italy's museums and churches—they were not always the savviest when it came to interpersonal skills. I had seen some who could hold a crowd in the palm of their hand as they weaved stories about 16th-century ceramics but couldn't hold your gaze when they ordered a drink.

But this one, this one was different. When Mike stayed at the bar with me while Monique and Maggie chatted, I tried to learn more.

"So… Nice that you have a friend visiting."

"The Magster? Yeah, she's a good egg," Mike said.

"In what way?" I asked in what I hoped was the most noncommittal tone possible.

"Well, she helped get me together with Kiki, for one."

It made me laugh that Mike's nickname for Monique was Kiki. She was so *not* a Kiki, with her tall, sophisticated (even a bit icy on the surface) appearance. On the other hand, it was hard not to notice the lusty looks they constantly gave each other, so maybe there was more Kiki in her than it would appear.

"Oh, how so?" I asked Mike as I handed yet another Aperol Spritz into waiting hands.

"Well, see, back in Berkeley, Maggie created this thing called the War Council."

"The War Council?"

"Yeah. We were like the A-Team of love." Mike let out a snort as he laughed about it.

"A-Team?"

"Or the squad from *Mission Impossible*. Basically, we found ways to fix people's love lives."

I wasn't sure what to think about that so I just said: "Sounds interesting."

"It was."

"Was?"

"Yeah, it disbanded. Well, it did for most of us anyway…"

Before I could ask any further questions, Professor Wilcox started gesturing that everyone should gather around so he could make his opening remarks. I watched as Wilcox and the tour director for the trip, Hilda, tussled over who should speak first. That didn't happen often, but I recalled it happening with this particular tour director the last time she led a group. She hadn't been to the hotel in a few years, but I knew she'd been in the travel industry for a long time, mostly because she started every conversation by letting me know. Let's just say the mileage was starting to show. Not so much in years or age but in an increasingly beleaguered and belligerent attitude toward the whole endeavor. The woman always appeared to be on the verge of a nervous breakdown, if you ask me. But nobody ever did ask me. That's the thing with bartenders and other service employees. Nobody asks us anything. We're invisible. Now, sometimes that's not a bad thing. It allowed me to see a lot more than most people realized without bringing any attention to myself. For a long time, that's how

I liked it. I wanted to be invisible. But with this group, especially with Mike and Monique's new friend along, maybe I didn't want to be quite so invisible.

Soon, the Berkeley group moved into the dining room for their welcome dinner. Once I closed up the bar, I headed home. When I walked by the town square, I saw, as usual, people in the cafes enjoying an *aperitivo*. In Italy, when you order a cocktail—often spritzes of one variety or another—you also get a tray of snacks. Depending on the establishment, they can range from potato chips and nuts to surprisingly high-quality cheese, salami, and olives. It's a very civilized custom, and I always felt it was too bad it hadn't been adopted back in the States, beyond the occasional stale pretzels and peanuts found in the dive-iest of bars. I passed all the happy-looking people and, for the first time in a long time, wished I had a group of people to meet for an *aperitivo*. My thoughts immediately returned to Mike, Monique, and their friend Maggie. But I shook those off. I barely knew them, and I had never mingled with the hotel guests—or even, really, the other hotel employees—before and didn't intend to start.

The next morning, I was back at the hotel early, as always, to provide the coffee-related drinks at the breakfast buffet. The hotel was hosting two smaller groups and the larger American one. I looked at the sheet the general manager had laid out for us. Table one had the eight Belgians, table two the ten Japanese, and tables three, four, and five the twenty-five Americans. I spotted Maggie as she came off the elevator. As she entered the breakfast room, she wore the telltale signs of jet lag coupled with confusion as to where she should sit.

"May I help you, signorina?" I said as she passed me.

"I'm looking for the UC Berkeley group?"

"You have those tables in the corner." I pointed to the tables already filling with other guests. "May I bring you some coffee or espresso?"

Maggie turned and looked at me as if I was throwing her a lifeline. "If it's possible, I would love a double or triple latte."

"You mean, two or three cups of milk?" I said, knowing what she meant but figuring I was providing an education into the ways of Italy.

"I'm sorry?"

"Latte means milk," I explained.

She laughed. "Got it. I want strong espresso-style coffee with a little milk and a spot of foam."

"One *doppio macchiato* coming up," I said with a smile.

"Bless you," she said with a caffeine-deprived smile of her own and a genuine look of gratitude in her eyes that made my heart skip a beat (a bit of a surprise to what I thought was a pretty dormant muscle).

Maggie was joined by the throngs of other guests, and I was slammed with orders for cappuccinos, macchiatos, espressos, and caffe—always say the caffe!—lattes, which I knew for them meant a great deal of foamy milk added to one espresso shot. Soon, the various tour directors called for their groups to congregate in the lobby, and they headed off on their tours—the Belgians and Japanese on coaches and the Americans walking to the harbor for their lake tour. The hotel grew quiet, and I had my four-hour break until early evening cocktail bar duty.

    I made my way through town, past the cafes and the cathedral, where I saw a number of the tour groups with their telltale flags, and the museum (same), and then into the botanical garden (yes, more groups there). As I passed through the west entrance to the garden, I peeked behind the gate. Once, while hiding from a woman I had briefly dated, I discovered a large wood carving featuring a faded painting hidden behind the branches and leaves. Quite different from the other art pieces found in the garden (predominantly sculptures), the painting depicted a young woman standing in front of a vineyard. Even if quite faded, the smile on the woman's face was mesmerizing and always brought a smile to my own face—as did seeing Signora Vitarelli later on in my walk. Well into her 80s and always elegantly dressed, Signora Vitarelli typically sat on a bench not far from the gate with her small and very furry dog that looked like a small mop sitting at her feet. It was her practice to take a *passeggiata* through the garden each morning around the time I headed home from my first shift at the hotel. In the afternoons, when I made my way back to the hotel, I would often find her at Pietro's cafe in the square having an *aperitivo*.

As usual, I stopped at the bench, offered her a slight bow and said, "*Buongiorno, Signora Vitarelli. È una bella giornata.*"

Signora Vitarelli smiled her demure smile, nodded graciously, and said, "*Si, Emilio, è vero,*" and I continued walking. I didn't know much about her beyond her name and the fact that her late husband had been a winemaker of some renown at one of the wineries outside of town. While her family still ran the winery, she chose to live in the city with her dog, who was so ancient and had such short legs that she often had to pick him up to walk even a few meters—transforming as he did from a mop into a winter muff like those designed to warm hands.

♡ ♥ ♡

On my walk through the garden the following day, moments after passing Signora Vitarelli, I spotted the UC Berkeley group. They were easy to recognize as some of them were wearing the dark-blue "Cal" caps I had seen Professor Wilcox hand out at the opening reception. They also wore lanyards holding sound systems that allowed them to listen to the tour guide. I looked over to see which local tour guide they had booked and spotted Bianca pointing toward a white lily, the national flower of Italy. Uh oh. I tried to look away so Bianca wouldn't see me, but it was too late. I gave what I considered to be my friendliest nod back in her direction, and she gave me a scowl before returning her attention to the group.

It was then that I noticed Maggie and Monique at the back of the group whispering to each other. Maggie seemed to have seen Bianca's scowl in my direction as she turned to look at me and offered a quizzical look. I offered a brief wave before quickly continuing on to my apartment. My sanctuary. I loved the small abode I had created for myself above the DeLuca's ceramics shop on a small side street in town. And yet, for some reason that day, my home did not provide the solace it usually did. I flopped down on my bed and thought about watching a film or reading a book, the two things I usually did with my free hours, but I felt kind of restless. I glanced at the computer on my desk that held my half-written dissertation, but that didn't really hold any allure either (and, to be honest, hadn't for a long time). Nothing did, so I just lay there in my ennui listening to the sounds of the DeLuca family having their lunch next door until it was time to go back to work.

On my afternoon walk back through the garden to the hotel, I was surprised to find Maggie standing near the West Gate—the same gate that covered the painting I'd always been curious about. As I got closer, I saw Maggie staring intently at the painting with her sunglasses held at her side.

"Did you lose your group?" I asked as I neared her.

"Huh?" she said, as if just noticing I was there. "Oh, yeah. I guess I did. They went back to the hotel. I just…"

"Had to come back and look at this?"

"I did. Is that weird?" Maggie turned and looked at me with those bright green eyes. Just mesmerizing.

"Not weird at all," I said. "I stop and look at it almost every day."

"You do?"

"I very much do," I said. I reached over and pulled back some of the branches that obscured the painting, and we both looked at it a little longer. I then looked at her. "I have to say… I mean, it is faded and all, but the woman in the painting, she looks a little like you."

"Okay. She does, doesn't she? I'm not crazy?"

"You are not … crazy." I don't know why I paused, but I did. It got a smile. I liked that.

"Do you know the artist?" Maggie asked.

"I do not. It was produced before my time. Way before my time. I heard somewhere that it was originally created for an international wine festival that was held in the region many decades ago." After we looked at the painting for a little longer, I added, "I might know some people who could provide more information, if you would like."

"That would be amazing…" Maggie turned to look at me. When she paused, I realized it was because she couldn't remember my name.

"Emilio," I said.

"Emilio," she said, nodding. "*Doppio macchiato* and Aperol Spritz Emilio, correct?"

"*Si. Eccomi.* That is me."

"Nice to meet you. Again." She offered her hand, which I took. Her skin was soft, but she had a firm grip. I liked that.

"And you are Maggie. Mike and Monique's friend Maggie."

"That I am."

We continued looking at the painting. Then Maggie put her sunglasses back on before breaking our silence. "So, how long has it been since you and Bianca were seeing each other?"

"I'm sorry?"

Maggie turned and peered at me over the sunglasses. "Bianca, our tour guide here in the botanical garden this morning."

"Oh, yes. Bianca. We weren't really seeing each other as much as…"

"Fuck buddies."

I laughed, but it was more out of embarrassment. "I'm sorry?"

Maggie gave me another look over her sunglasses. "I think you know."

"We had a very casual understanding."

"Sorry, dude, but based on what I saw earlier today, it was not casual for her."

"I…" I then realized Maggie might be right. I hadn't meant to hurt Bianca. I mean, she was a lovely gal, but we went out for maybe two months at the beginning of the year, and I never saw things turning into anything beyond the informal "dates" (I refused to call it fuck buddies) we had been enjoying. Truthfully, our casual understanding (I also refused to call it a relationship) had been over for a while. I told Bianca that—in person, even—but she had trouble accepting it. So I did my best to avoid her. Unfortunately, I couldn't help but occasionally run into Bianca or pass in close proximity to her. Part of the problem with living in a smaller city and both being involved in the tourism industry was the difficulty in disentangling. At least she was originally from the Puglia region far to the south, so I didn't have to worry about running into any irate family members as well.

Instead of saying all of that, I said, "If you would like, I would be happy to help you find the artist who painted this picture."

"I would like that." Maggie smiled. And what a smile it was. And then she asked the funniest question: "So, what's the deal with the dogs in this town?"

Chapter Seven
MAGGIE

Yeah, I asked Emilio about the dogs. Can you believe he never noticed? How can you live in a town with the Westminster Dog Show going on outside your door every damn day and not notice? Other than his obliviousness to that fact, I have to say Emilio was okay. Definitely not bad on the eyes, although he appeared to know that. Based on the description of his dalliance with Bianca, Emilio also appeared to be the type that felt better about his lack of ability to commit by considering himself a serial monogamist. I'd seen the type before—a lot—including with my most recent boyfriend, Nick, he of the War Council set-up. I had learned recently that Nick stayed in France after his year abroad, teaching English and dating a gallery owner. It didn't surprise me. Nick was one of those men who liked having a steady gal by his side, so when I didn't go to join him, I knew he would find someone else. Hearing about the new girlfriend wasn't as hard on me as I might have expected. In fact, it only solidified he wasn't "the one," if "the one" existed, at least for me. The problem with having a superpower that allows you to read people well (not to mention the overall opinion that the human race sucks) is that it can kind of screw up your own interpersonal relationships.

But, as I said, Emilio was not bad in the looks department. Tall, he had wavy brown hair that had a tendency to fall in front of his soft brown eyes and long, thin fingers that he used to brush the hair away when he turned to look at me—a motion that was somehow incredibly sexy. Yum. If he really had called things off with Bianca, the very entertaining local guide who gave him the gaze-of-death during our tour of the garden, maybe we could even have a little fling. Something about arriving in Italy had reignited my libido. Maybe it was those darn spritzes. Either way, I was grateful to know I could feel a little something in that department again. I could see why Mike and Monique were horny little rabbits here, although to be fair, that was true for them back in Berkeley, too.

Anyway, Emilio was definitely the best-looking—and most interesting—of the men I had met so far. A quick scan of those of the male persuasion that had come across my path in those first few days included Rodrigo, the concierge, who was too mousy; Vincenzo, the bus driver who was way too old and crotchety for me; Matteo, the bellman who was too… too… just not for me. Anyway, you get the picture. Even as fling material, they lacked. But not Emilio. He had promise. Might be just what the doctor ordered, as they say. A little non-committal affair to get me out of my doldrums before returning to my life in Berkeley.

Why not? Right?

But only if he had truly cut things off with Bianca. I definitely did not want to get in the middle of that triangle. Can you get in the middle of a triangle? Seems like the borders would keep you out. But I digress. In the meantime, the little flirtation we had going would suffice. Not to mention, I really did want to learn more about the artwork in the botanical garden. I found it fascinating and not just because I looked like the woman in the piece. I sent a picture to Kathy, and even she responded by asking if I had a secret life I hadn't told her about, you know, 65 years ago (the date we found listed on the painting). Plus, I figured that Emilio might help me find the answer to the dog question. I really was curious about the dog obsession in Lacusara.

Other than my burgeoning flirtation with Emilio, my first few days in Italy were spent getting to know the cast of characters on the tour. With 25, it made it harder to pick out everyone's traits quickly like I could with smaller groups. Besides, Monique and I had our hands full with the main issue affecting the trip so far: tempering the competing personalities of Professor Wilcox and Hilda, the tour director. It reminded me of situations where a CEO hired me to examine their board or a set of employees only for me to determine the CEO was the cause of the dysfunction. Wilcox and Hilda weren't bad on their own. More like little gnats buzzing around with their constant bickering. I'll admit I kind of started out on the side of Hilda. Abrasive personality aside, she was just trying to keep us organized after all.

Although Monique was right and Wilcox had mellowed from the bellicose individual I remembered, I could see he harbored a great deal of anger and resentment. Much of it was likely the result of losing his wife, who Monique told me had been a gem. The two of them never had any children, and her death followed a long battle with cancer. A year and a half later, that anger and sorrow and solitude seemed to be manifesting itself in a lot of alpha dog tussling with Hilda. There didn't seem to be any actual elbows thrown, but metaphorical ones were definitely bandied about. In his defense, Hilda wasn't making it easy on him. Again, although her intentions were good—organization!—she reminded me of those flight attendants who had logged way too many hours and at a certain point just didn't give a damn. They go through the motions but with a rigidity verging on nastiness that ruins the experience. It didn't help that Hilda hadn't overseen this particular trip in several years, and it wasn't following the usual structure. Leaving things loose clearly wasn't in Hilda's personal wheelhouse. This being my first trip, I didn't know the difference, but I could sense the displeasure she felt at opening up a schedule that hadn't changed in years. Hilda obviously thrived on creating order out of the chaos of travel. As someone who adored organization and rules and routines, I could relate, but I also wasn't in charge, merely a bystander. So, again, while they both had their reasons, that didn't negate the effect their bickering might have on the group. If we wanted to keep the group happy, Monique and I might have to spring into action.

Monique and I first diagnosed their conflict at the dinner that followed the opening reception. Held in the hotel's restaurant, located adjacent to the lobby, the dinner was … fine. The meal I'd had earlier that day in the cafe tasted much better than one provided by a hotel that caters to tour groups. I totally understood why. Feeding a couple dozen people all at once is more of a challenge than crafting individual dishes. It also underscored why attempting to tailor trips for larger groups to help them explore the "real" Italy–the stated goal of adding days to this trip– might be difficult. With such a large group, how could a bespoke experience be created? As one who was just learning about the country (and the tourism industry) myself, I didn't have any answers. What I did have answers for–my "superpower" as Monique liked to call it–was troubleshooting difficult groups. Or, in this case, difficult group leaders.

At the dinner, I sat with Mike and Monique. Well, I did after the two of them returned following the need to "step outside" to make a "phone call." Ha. They weren't fooling anyone. Or, at least, they weren't fooling me. Mike's shirt tail wasn't completely tucked in when they got back, and although Monique's red lipstick had been perfectly re-applied, her mane of blonde hair had an errant luggage tag stuck to the back. *Rabbits*, I laughed to myself as I discreetly removed it. But good for them.

While waiting for Mike and Monique to return, I scanned the crowd. As I mentioned to Monique at the reception, the whole group radiated a quality best described as "earnest." You know, pleasant, well-meaning sorts. From the oldest couple still holding hands to the youngest woman happily conversing with the people at her table, they appeared quite agreeable. I'd say nauseatingly so, except that I was trying to be good. I then spied the man who had kept to himself at both the airport and the welcome reception at the far end of the table. I took a closer look (surreptitiously, of course) at "Clark" (according to his nametag). Ah, so that was Clark (he of the lack of picture and bio in the pre-trip materials). His demeanor appeared perfectly amiable on the surface. Verging on bland, Clark had the black-rimmed glasses, short-cropped hair, button-down shirt, and khaki pant uniform

♡ *The Italy Affair* ♡

of most middle-aged white men. I still sensed an underlying belligerence. Clark solidified my diagnosis when, just before Mike and Monique returned, he decided to let everyone at the table know that the pasta was not, in fact, as "al dente" as it should have been. That was it. Only words he uttered all meal. The rest of us at the table merely nodded and offered polite smiles before returning to our own conversations.

Following Mike and Monique's return, the three of us watched Wilcox and Hilda make the rounds of the tables. Hilda was telling the couples and other people traveling together about the local restaurant options they could choose from on their free nights in town so she could make the necessary reservations. Wilcox, on the other hand, was offering an introduction to the history of the art in the towns we would be visiting along the lake the next day. All well and good, but occasionally they would reach the same table and bring out those metaphorical elbows when regaling the guests with their spiels. At that point, Monique and I made eye contact while nodding in their direction. Yep, they needed help. Time to bring in the War Council.

♡ ♥ ♡

The following day on our first excursion—a boat ride along the expansive lake—the conflict between Wilcox and Hilda became even more apparent. The day started with everyone meeting in the lobby at 8:30 sharp to walk over to the harbor and catch our charter boat. *Why, in god's name, do we have to start this early?* My jet-lagged brain kept screaming in my ear, even if I—and Hilda—happily noted that everyone was on time. Well, except for Clark, who leisurely walked out of the hotel at 8:37 and glared at everyone as if to say, "Oh yeah, you had to wait for me. So what?" Luckily, with the rest of the group's genial nature, it caused barely a ripple as they happily continued chatting amongst themselves. Hilda noticed. I noticed. They did not.

Once on the boat, we disembarked at a few of the adorable towns lining the lake. At each, Professor Wilcox would attempt to point out something of interest. Then Hilda would interrupt him to let everyone know how much time they had in the town and exactly when they had to be back on the boat. We visited five towns, and it happened at every single one.

At the fifth town, Monique and I solidified our decision to use some of our War Council techniques on them. Not full War Council. I mean, the War Council was created for romantic relationships (which this was most definitely not) and a complete tactical team (which we were most definitely not). In this case, we had a communications expert and a sociologist hoping to help some people in need. We might as well use our skills for good, right? That's what we told ourselves anyway. It's not like we could lecture on the artwork or history of the town or handle the logistics of international travel. This was what Beverly sent us to do, right?

As always, the first step involved research. With Mike back at the rugby camp, that fell to Monique and me. We decided that we would begin the following day during our tour of Lacusara. As much as I would have preferred to do otherwise (since I really did admire Hilda's attempt to create order out of the chaos of corralling more than two dozen people, even if her demeanor could use some work), we decided that I would start with Wilcox, and Monique would take Hilda to learn what personality traits or personal history we might be able to leverage. Monique made the point that her history with Wilcox and my affinity toward Hilda's methods meant we should swap positions. I begrudgingly admitted she was right.

Our tour of Lacusara again began with the group gathering in the lobby at 8:30 sharp. Still earlier than necessary (in my opinion), but at least the jet lag had started to abate, so it wasn't quite as painful as the first day. Once assembled, we would walk into town, through the botanical gardens, and over to the cathedral. Once I had my *doppio macchiato* (thank you, Emilio with the beautiful hair and hands for introducing me to those!), I was ready.

At the entrance to the botanical garden, we met our local guide, Bianca, a tiny spitfire of a gal who spoke in a rapid Italian-infused English.

She told us the history of the garden, which had been created in secret by locals during World War II and lovingly maintained ever since. As we began our walk through the garden, I nodded to Monique, who was standing next to Hilda, and made my way over to Wilcox.

"It is a beautiful garden," I said, using the most boring conversation starter ever.

"Indeed," said Wilcox. "I always enjoy my constitutionals through the flora here."

Interesting way to say a walk through the flowers, but heck, I was used to intellectual babble after a dozen years in academia.

"The history is so interesting as well," I said as Bianca pointed to a white lily and identified it as the national flower of Italy. "And the sculptures."

"Indeed."

"Is that part of your area of expertise?"

"No," he said, looking at the modern sculptures we were passing. "My realm goes much further back to the late Renaissance artists that followed Da Vinci and Michelangelo—particularly Paolo Luciano, a transformational figure in the art world in his time. As you are no doubt aware, he was born nearby in Bonvini and started the art academy in Verniciara."

"Fascinating."

"Unfortunately, Luciano is considered a bit archaic these days. Like me, I suppose."

If that wasn't the saddest thing I'd heard. "I don't think that's true, Professor Wilcox." I noticed that he didn't correct my usage of his last name instead of his first. With our age difference, it felt appropriate.

He gave me a rueful look. "Oh, my dear, I'm afraid it is. People will always speak of Michelangelo and Da Vinci, but Paolo Luciano has been relegated to obsolete tomes like mine that aren't even used in introductory art history courses anymore."

"And yet you are so popular on these tours, Professor."

Wilcox looked at me with rueful eyes. "That's sweet, but as I'm sure you have noticed, even in this group, the only people interested in my work are those closest to my age." He pointed to the cute older couple and a few others of similar vintage walking behind the rest of the group who were bounding about taking pictures and excitedly talking to Bianca about this flower and that. "And I'm not even allowed to show them the parts of Bonvini that would truly interest those who enjoy Luciano's work when we visit there tomorrow."

"Why is that?"

"We can't please everyone, my dear. There just isn't enough time for side trips to the foundry or his birthplace while also getting in the duomo and visiting newer artists." He sighed. "It's fine. The truth is, without my wife Doris with me, I'm just an old bore."

"Oh, Professor Wilcox, please don't say that."

"It's an accurate assessment. I am not incognizant of the fact that Doris created a more ebullient atmosphere on these trips. She made every day a little brighter for everyone around her. Now, even these beautiful flowers can't brighten mine."

My heart broke for the man. Just broke. It was then I saw the older woman with the Pekinese dog—a.k.a. the furry footstool—that I had noticed in the cafe on my first day. *Was that only two days ago? This jet lag really is a doozy.* Again dressed to the nines (she even wore gloves), she sat on a bench off to the side of the garden with her dog at her feet, smiling as sweetly as she had at the cafe that first day. I wondered if the cafe was her next stop. Then it occurred to me that she looked to be about the same age as Wilcox. The man's wife had been gone for almost two years now, perhaps he might enjoy meeting a new friend... It didn't have to be romantic... I shook my head. I was contemplating setting Wilcox up with an Italian woman I didn't even know when my real War Council mission was to coax him into getting along with Hilda. Silly me.

I gave Wilcox a sympathetic pat on the shoulder and rejoined Monique off to the side of the group. It was then I observed our hotel bartender Emilio on the far side of the garden. As he walked by the older woman with the dog, he stopped to talk to her for a moment. (How sweet was that?) When he turned slightly to look in our direction, I observed our local guide Bianca shooting him hate-filled daggers (metaphorical, of course, but compelling nonetheless) from her eyes. Before Emilio could turn back and pretend not to notice her, he was caught. He gave Bianca a slight nod. Then he saw Monique and me and offered a little wave, which we returned. *What an interesting interaction!* I thought as we continued the tour.

Later, as we exited through the walls that surrounded the botanical garden, I discovered the painting that piqued my curiosity. While everybody else followed Bianca—she of the chipper patter and dagger-like gaze at our hotel bartender—through the gate that led into the heart of the city, I stopped to hold the gate farther back to let everyone through. As I did, I looked behind it at the wall that encased the garden and thought I spotted a faded splotch of blue. Strange. I pulled the foliage away and found a large work of art affixed to the side of the wall. I couldn't tell if it was a carving of a painting or a painting on a carving. Either way, it appeared to be quite old. Still, amid the faded paint and foliage encasing it, a picture—that of a young woman—remained visible. Barely. It was as if Mother Nature was slowly erasing her existence.

When I looked closer, I noticed the woman in the picture had long black hair not unlike mine. While I usually kept my hair pulled back with a barrette or headband, hers flowed around her shoulders, and she wore a faded blue dress similar in color to one I had brought on the trip with me. The woman held one hand to her heart while the other held a clump of grapes attached to a series of vines hovering in the air above her shoulder. But it was her smile that entranced me. I mean, it wasn't the Mona Lisa's enigmatic smile. It was more... *What was the word? Not happy, something more than that... Not exuberant... Not...* As I pondered, I noticed Wilcox passing behind me with the slower members of the group.

"Professor Wilcox," I asked, "do you know this piece?"

"Ah. No. I have not observed this before." He stepped in and looked at it a little closer. "Rather interesting, is it not?"

"Rather," I said, using his lexicon. *Why the hell not, right?*

"You know," he said after a few moments, "it resembles a painting I heard chatter about some years ago that was created for a harvest festival the town hosted. That would have been around the mid-1900s, not long after the creation of this garden. It doesn't date back as far as Paolo Luciano, of course, but it shares some of the qualities he was known for. It could have been created by someone who attended the art academy Luciano founded in Verniciara, which we will be visiting in a few days."

Wilcox brushed some leaves aside and took a more lingering look. "While I can't pinpoint the artist, I seem to recall some discussion as to its origin." He looked back at me. "Faded as it is, the painting reveals a great deal of raw emotion, don't you think? Especially when compared to the more sterile pieces that have been placed much more prominently in the botanical garden. Regardless of its provenance, the painter had a great deal of skill, and I would hazard a guess that the woman depicted here was very much loved."

Wow. I was quite impressed with the depth of his analysis. "Thank you, Professor Wilcox."

A great deal of raw emotion, I thought as I took one last look and then hurried to catch up to the group. Was that what was speaking to me? The raw emotion? That wasn't really the descriptor I would have used for the woman's smile, but I still couldn't quite figure out what I would use. As I followed the group through our tour of the city, I decided to make a point to check the painting out in more depth later.

During the rest of the tour, we saw and learned more about the cathedral (gorgeous), opera house (ditto), and the textile museum, among other sites. Okay, I'll admit a lot went in one ear and out the other. Then, we were given free time for lunch. Before letting us go, Bianca suggested a few places we might enjoy. Hilda added that after lunch we could stay and continue to explore the town on our own or walk back to the hotel. People began to scatter. As part of the plan Monique and I concocted, I stayed with Wilcox for lunch while Monique went with Hilda. Before we parted, I quickly mentioned to Monique that part of Wilcox's issues seemed to have to do with feeling irrelevant. Monique

♡ Maggie ♡

nodded and said she'd hopefully learn more from Hilda at lunch.

I joined Wilcox and his fans, a.k.a. the older folks who admired him the most, for a short while at lunch. When they started reminiscing about attractions they'd seen on previous trips, I excused myself and made my way back to the botanical garden. I wanted to take another look at the art piece before heading back to the hotel for a little rest and the early evening lecture.

Needless to say, I was surprised to run into Emilio in the garden and even more surprised by his offer to help me find out more about the story behind the artwork. How fun to have a new Italian adventure, in addition (of course) to our covert War Counciling of Wilcox and Hilda!

Chapter Eight
MONIQUE

I started wondering if using War Council techniques on Professor Wilcox and Hilda was such a good idea, even if we were still only in the research stage. It's not as if a detente of any sort had occurred. No, the two of them seemed to hate each other more than ever. It's more that once I got past her decidedly combative demeanor, I started to sympathize with Hilda. Maggie seemed to feel the same about Wilcox. I suppose those were natural reactions on our part since our stated goal was, after all, to help them and that required a bit of empathy. Interestingly, from what Maggie told me just before my lunch with Hilda after our tour of Lacusara, their issues sounded quite similar. The root of their conflict originated from their inability to give everyone the type of tour they desired: Wilcox wanted to give everyone at least a modicum of context to the sights while Hilda was set on making sure they saw everything as efficiently as possible.

When dealing with a sizeable group, which by its very nature moves slower, you can only see so much. And yet, when it comes to traveling, groups have some advantages over individuals—pre-arranged plans and reservations often moved them to the front of lines or in to see unique offerings. But how to offer the best of both worlds? Was it possible?

I also noted that Maggie started to be distracted by Emilio, of all people. Yes, Emilio presented an attractive countenance. In every aesthetic metric, the man received high marks—one of the reasons for his popularity with all the gals in town, I presumed. I'd seen him rotate through a few of them in the two summers I had spent at the hotel. That wasn't the problem. The problem was that the man was… How shall I put this…? Undirected. Probably one of the reasons why his relationships never lasted. I mean, the man was obviously dealing with *things*. Mike mentioned Emilio confiding in him regarding his divorce and his departure from a doctoral program in Florence, so I could only surmise that perhaps he was hiding out a bit. Pouring drinks to anonymous tour groups was as good a way to hide as any, I suppose.

What did that have to do with Maggie? I wasn't entirely sure. I mean, if Maggie was attracted to him, good for her. Although it seemed out of character for her, perhaps an Italian affair would be beneficial—especially after all she had been through the last few years with

Bill and Nick and the War Council. I didn't worry about her ending up like Bianca and wishing to annihilate Emilio. (Yes, I understood the Italian curse words Bianca muttered every time she saw him. I had heard them enough when watching Mike's rugby games.) Besides, Maggie was only here for another week—and on a group trip—so there was only so much canoodling (if indeed that ended up occurring) that could be done. Canoodling. I got a smile on my face as I wondered where Mike might be at that moment.

But my project was not Maggie and Emilio. It was Hilda, so I kept my focus on her. I had started by attempting to gain Hilda's trust, primarily by posing questions about her job while we walked through Lacusara. I then broached the idea of sharing a meal during the break.

"Why don't we have lunch together, Hilda? I'd love to continue to learn more about the intricacies of your position here."

"That's hard to believe, but whatever, sure," Hilda said.

"Wonderful! Do you have a favorite restaurant?"

"There's one where the local guides like to eat, away from the tourists."

"Sounds lovely."

"I might need to make a few calls or texts while we eat, though," Hilda said, peering into her phone again.

Way to sell it, Hilda. Way to sell it. "Not a problem." I smiled sweetly in an attempt to mimic Maggie's appeasement techniques.

We found a seat at a utilitarian-looking spot in an alley off the main square. Hilda wasn't wrong about it being a favorite among the guides as I recognized Bianca, the local guide we had met in the botanical garden (she of the obscenity muttering toward Emilio), among a half dozen others I'd worked with before. Interesting. It also appeared popular among the bus drivers as I spotted our burly bus driver Vincenzo, who played in the senior rugby league out at the sports facility. I suppose this made the restaurant the equivalent of the local travel industry's clubhouse. The food consisted of basic Italian fare but cooked well and, perhaps most importantly, fast and cheap. The meal came with a pint of Peroni beer, the beverage of choice for lunch in these parts, and seemingly a must for the guides after a morning spent corralling clueless tourists. Not the case for the drivers, I happily noted, as I gave Vincenzo a little wave as he took a swig from a bottle of mineral water.

"So, tell me about these trips," I started after we had been served.

"What do you want to know?" Hilda asked curtly, shoveling the food into her mouth in a most unappealing way.

"You've been leading them for some time, no?"

"Forever," she said, rolling her eyes. "Not this one, though. Gabriella usually leads it, but she took this year off after having her baby." Hilda practically snorted the word "baby" as if it were an obscenity.

"I see," I said, deciding not to mention that Mike and I had been pondering the concept ourselves.

"Don't think I don't know what I'm doing, though," she said. "I led this one five years ago."

A lot has happened in five years, I thought. Instead, I said, "And yet the university has changed things up a bit this year, no?"

She shot me a look. "I know what I'm doing," she snapped.

"I didn't mean to imply otherwise," I said, trying desperately to regain control of the conversation. *Why, oh why, did I tell Maggie she could take Wilcox? He is a lamb compared to this woman.* "I'm just saying that adding the extra days changes things up a bit."

Hilda grunted. "I know what I'm doing," she said again, but quieter.

"See, and I do not," I said, attempting to appeal to her egocentric way of viewing the world. "And I'm an academic, so I love learning about, well, everything, I suppose. I'm curious, at what point do you become involved?"

"Not early enough," she said, sighing. "Everything had already been planned when they brought me in, much of it badly because of the changes in the schedule this year."

"For instance?"

"For instance, yesterday we took the lake tour. That's fine, but we really should have started with the tour of this city. It's closest to our hotel, so by giving the guests an awareness of their surroundings, they would already have a sense of where they'd like to go on their free evenings."

I hadn't thought of that. "Good point," I said. "Who makes those kinds of decisions?"

"The truth? Usually some young dolt back in the home office who's never done the tour before. They give them a template from previous trips and go from there."

"But why?"

Hilda shrugged. "They're cheap." More shoveling of food. Really, the woman could use some tips on how to eat in a more civilized manner. I was going to say "attractive," but "civilized" is more accurate. Aesthetics had nothing to do with it, except for the rather grotesque images now burned into my brain. Still, Hilda had a point, and it became more evident why she was so cranky all the time. (No excuse for the poor eating habits.)

"And, okay," Hilda acknowledged between bites, "sometimes it's availability. The boat excursions don't run every day, and on Sundays, some of the churches aren't available for tours so things might need to be juggled. But that wasn't the case here. We should start at the hotel and radiate out with our tours to give people a sense of place."

I nodded. Made sense. "They don't take your insights into consideration at all?"

Hilda snorted. Really, most unattractive. Sorry, uncivilized. Then she said, "In this case, the insights would come from Gabriella since she usually leads this tour. In general, though, we don't really have time to give them. I'm only contracted for the months I'm on the ground. We send notes at the end of each trip on how to improve the next one, but who knows if anyone actually reads them, or better yet, incorporates them?"

"What trips do you typically lead?"

"The Alps region—Swiss, Austrian, Italian, and German. They're closer to my home on the other side of the border near Lake Lugano."

"Oh, so you are Swiss?" I asked, thinking she was one of the most un-Swiss-like people I had ever met (based solely on archetypal stereotypes and the few I'd met at academic conferences, of course).

Hilda rolled her eyes. "Yes," she said as if it was the stupidest question in the world. She paused and put down her fork at last, although she didn't wipe off the red sauce that had become attached to her face. I tried my best to look around it, but that verged on impossible. "Okay, I'm going to bottom line it for you," she continued. "Here's what I have learned in more than 20 years of doing this: Some people love rules and schedules. They love being told what to do, following where they are led, and seeing everything they've heard about. The only way to get those people into everything is to stay on a regimented schedule. We need to start early so we can get the best views and won't have to tussle with the crowds. Fine. They give me a schedule. I make sure we follow that schedule."

Hilda finally wiped her face with her napkin (thank god) and took a swig of her Peroni. I readied myself for a belch that never came (again, thank god). If it had, I might have stopped our little experiment right then and there. Instead, she continued: "Others, well, they don't necessarily feel the same way. They came on the trip because they've always wanted to see the destination and this tour fit the bill. Or they wanted someone else to plan their trip for them. But they would prefer experiencing a few things instead of running through everything available. Either way, there's always a tug of war between the ones who want to see it all in a regimented way and the ones who want more flexibility."

"Interesting."

"You betcha. We're dealing with people, after all. People who by their very nature can be…"

"Challenging," I offered.

"Exactly," she said, tapping her index finger on her nose, which only added more red sauce to her face. *Really, woman, must you?!* "The truth is that some—a lot, really—don't know what they want until they get here. On paper, all the activities sound great, but once they're here, getting to sleep in and spending the day sitting in a cafe sipping on a spritz might sound better."

"There isn't just one Italy for everybody."

Hilda again touched her index finger to her nose, this time feeling the red sauce and using her napkin to wipe it off (thankfully). "Exactly," she said, not skipping a beat. "Italy is museums and churches. Italy is also spending three-hour lunches with friends. Italy is wandering through vineyards… or learning to make pasta or…"

"Or playing rugby all day." Hilda gave me a look. "My husband runs the summer rugby camps in Bonvini," I explained.

Hilda laughed. Snorted, really. "Or playing rugby all day." Then she sighed. "With the parameters they give me, I can only do the first one. Regimented stops at all the sights."

"I wondered about that… What if there was a way to offer more?"

I understood the beleaguered look this idea brought to Hilda's face. She was used to people having grand ideas that she would end up having to implement. Before she could get angry and say it wasn't possible, I continued: "No, hear me out. This particular trip was given extra days because people were asking for more time to, as the name indicates, immerse themselves in Italy. To do some of those activities you mentioned. While we still have the traditional tour framework, we also have a little more free time. And you have more help than usual, so why not open it up a little? I mean, you have

Professor Wilcox…" Hilda sighed. "But you also have Maggie and me along to assist. Since we have more time built in for people to see the Italy they want to see, what if we…"

My mind raced trying to figure out what that might be. "What if, say, we split into smaller groups for tomorrow's activities with each of us taking lead on one of them?"

"Tomorrow, we're scheduled for a tour of the town you just mentioned, Bonvini."

"Right. And that's my town—well, the town I've spent the last three summers in—and the hometown of the Renaissance artist Wilcox is an expert on. It's also home to the rugby camp and surrounded by some lovely wineries. Obviously, we can't offer everyone all of those activities, but what if we offered people a few options of how they'd like to spend their day there?"

"I don't know…"

"What's the harm in trying it? Just one day."

Hilda took another swig of her beer and looked at me, narrowing her eyes as she did. I'm sure she was gauging how much extra work it would be for her and whether it would be worth it. Finally, she said, "If you can get everyone on board, I suppose we could give it a try."

"Great!" I said and then immediately wondered what I had gotten myself into. When I met with Cal's alumni travel director, Beverly, she had asked me to find ways to improve the trip. I suppose this sufficed, but we were adding these options on the fly, and I hadn't received any permission.

That evening, following Professor Wilcox's lecture on Paolo Luciano, we gathered for a group dinner at a local restaurant in the hills above the hotel. There, Hilda, Maggie, and I started polling the participants on how they might like to spend their day in Bonvini. As I had presumed, they fell into a few camps. One group wanted the original guided tour that included all of the highlights of the town with a local guide, which had already been set up and could be overseen by Hilda. One group said they preferred to spend more time at the sites related to the artist Paolo Luciano, which Professor Wilcox could lead. To my surprise, a few actually did want to check out the rugby camp. I knew Mike had an amateur-level group of adults that week so it wouldn't be a problem accommodating a few extra. The rest indicated they would prefer to spend the day touring the wineries just outside town. I could take the sports group (hello equipment room!) and put Maggie in charge of the wineries. We could still have Vincenzo, the driver, drop us all off and pick us up at the same time, but once on site, we could provide four different adventures that satisfied each person's desires.

What could go wrong?

Chapter Nine
EMILIO

In an interesting turn of events—and with the hotel's *consenso* (approval)—I ended up joining the travel group from UC Berkeley on their tour of the town of Bonvini. I wasn't scheduled for the breakfast shift that day, and I assured my manager that I would be back in plenty of time to set up the bar for the cocktail hour at 5 p.m. Maggie had invited me to join them when the group returned from their dinner the night before. She found me closing up the bar, and I was able to tell her that I learned from my general manager that a winery out near Bonvini had spearheaded the international wine festival for which the painting in the garden was reportedly created. Maggie then told me that Monique had fiddled with their schedule a bit, and she would be leading the group visiting three wineries the next day, and maybe we could learn more from one of them. Maggie figured (rightly so) that having an interpreter on hand to talk with the winery owners might be helpful.

Monique's adjustment of the group's itinerary intrigued me. I mean, it wasn't a huge shift. Their original schedule had them visiting Bonvini, albeit on a more typical (and formal) tour using a local guide. While those tours included free time for lunch or shopping or maybe even a stop at one of the wineries, the group would be moving en masse, which invariably leads to the loss of time for extras. In general, the bigger the group, the slower they move. It's physics. I guess. As someone who studied film, who was I to say?

Anyway, by splitting up the group, people would be able to see certain things in more detail and, ideally, see them alongside those who moved at a similar tempo. I wasn't sure how they got the tour operator (especially with a tour director like Hilda) to go along with it, but it sounded intriguing. From what Maggie told me, one group would be going for a slower walk through the part of town that held all the hometown inspirations for the artist Paolo Luciano with Professor Wilcox offering lectures along the way. The second group would join Hilda and the local guide for the originally scheduled tour of the town. The third group would be going with Monique out to the sports complex where Mike held his rugby camps. It made me laugh thinking about that one, even though only four of them chose to participate, and they did look the most athletically inclined. To add a cultural element, Mike's assistant coach, Fabrizio, would offer language lessons. That made me laugh even harder, knowing the kind of language Fabrizio tended to use. The fourth group, the one Maggie would be leading (with me tagging along), would tour three area wineries, including (we hoped) the one instrumental in organizing the international wine festival all those years ago. At Monique's suggestion, the plan was to visit the wineries via e-bike, which made sense for navigating the narrow (and very hilly) country roads that surrounded the town.

It felt strange the following morning at 8:30 a.m. to be boarding the coaches I saw groups troop on and off of every day in front of the hotel. I gave the bus driver Vincenzo an embarrassed wave as I stepped by. Down the row, I saw Maggie with an empty seat next to her.

As I walked past the first few rows, I heard someone say, "*Buongiorno*, Emilio. Are you joining us today?"

"I am, Signor Thompson," I said, talking to the charming older gentleman who always ordered two *vini bianchi* for him and his wife and told me they were celebrating their 65th wedding anniversary on the trip.

"Isn't that lovely?" Signor Thompson said. "Isn't that lovely, dear?"

"It really is," Signora Thompson said sweetly. "Just lovely." I noticed they were holding hands. Sixty-five years together and still holding hands. How could you not love that?

When I reached Maggie's row, I asked, "May I?"

"Of course!" she said, patting the seat next to her.

"We can go over some of the logistics," I said, as if I had to justify sitting beside her. What was I: twelve?

As I sat down next to Maggie, I felt a few *farfalle nello stomaco* (butterflies in my stomach). Ever since I'd found Maggie standing in front of the painting in the botanical garden, my attraction to her had only increased. Yes, I noticed her physical appeal at the first reception. She had a *Bringing Up, Baby*-era Katharine Hepburn quality I tended to find irresistible. So there was already that. But I also loved the way her mind worked. For instance, her comment about the variety of dogs in Lacusara. I'm going to be honest that I had never noticed. I sure did now. I had even started counting them during my daily walks and was up to a dozen different breeds. I wasn't sure how to take it that Maggie found it a character flaw in me that I hadn't noticed them before. Then again, I've often been accused of being off in my own little dream world, whereas she seemed to notice *everything*—even picking up on the fact that Bianca hated me with a passion from all the way across the garden. Made me a little nervous, if you must know the truth. More *farfalle nello stomaco*.

We stepped off the bus at the edge of Bonvini and split into our designated groups. Hilda stridently took her crew—the largest at about ten—to meet the local guide holding the requisite flag to take them on the scheduled tour of the city. Professor Wilcox walked slowly with the Thompsons and the other (older, slower) art lovers in the direction of the small museum built at the birthplace of Paolo Luciano. Monique took the four sports fanatics off in the opposite direction toward the athletic field. I noticed some couples de-coupling for their tours, the sports nuts giving their spouses a little kiss on the cheek before sprinting back toward Monique with an excitement I hadn't seen on their faces since they arrived.

    Maggie and I took the six who wanted to visit the wineries to the bike shop, where we received our e-bikes and set out on our adventure. I noted that the members of our group were on the younger side (which in this group meant 40s and 50s) and more active—if maybe not as athletic (or crazy) as those choosing to spend the day playing rugby. Still, we had what I would call the cool kids, if that's still a thing. Hilda and Monique had already informed the winery owners that we were coming. An optional visit to a local winery during the free time in the afternoon had always been part of the original itinerary, so they just expanded that by letting all three know the approximate time our group of eight would be showing up on our bikes. To help out with the timing, I called ahead before we reached each winery so they could have the tasting set up. I just hoped the group wouldn't get too boisterous. That occasionally happened at the wine-tasting events we held at the hotel.

All in all, we had a lovely day. Everyone stayed on their best behavior, although I noticed by the third winery their voices were getting a little louder—a by-product of the wine tastings plus a day spent bonding on the bikes. At each stop, while the others enjoyed their tastings, Maggie and I would find the winery managers or owners and show them the pictures of the artwork we had taken on our phones. We didn't have any luck showing the pictures at the first two wineries. Although long-established wineries, both had new owners—young former city dwellers trying their hands at viticulture. At the third one, once the young tasting room manager set the group up with their first round of wines, we pulled her aside and showed her the picture. She squinted a bit at it and called out to someone in the back.

"*Gianpaolo, vieni qui.*"

A jovial-looking man came through a door in the back and stood behind a large bar. "*Che cosa, Stefania?*"

Stefania pointed at us, and we walked up to meet him at the bar while she returned to the wine tasters.

"*Buona sera,*" he said to Maggie and me. "*Posso aiutarla?*"

"*Buona sera, signore. Parla inglese?*" I asked, nodding to Maggie.

"Yes, I speak a little," Gianpaolo said. "How may I assist?"

"My name is Emilio, and this is Margherita," I said, using the Italian version of Maggie's name. She gave me a funny look, but I thought it appropriate with a man this formal. "She is part of the tour group from the University of California." I pointed to the group sitting at the table behind us. They had a series of red wine-filled glasses laid out before them with Stefania holding the bottle up for everyone to see.

"Ah, yes. I was told you might come by today," Gianpaolo said. "I believe your group will be visiting us again in a few days for the cooking class my wife teaches over at the villa."

That was news to me, so I looked at Maggie, who nodded. "I guess we are then," I said.

Gianpaolo smiled. Maggie smiled. Smiles all around. "We did have a question for you, though, today," I continued. "In the Lacusara botanical garden the other day, we saw a wine-themed artwork and were curious about its provenance."

"Provenance?" he asked.

"*Provenienza*," I clarified. "Its history. Why it was created. We heard the painting might have been commissioned for a wine festival held in the area."

"This area did hold the International Viticulture Festival once, but that was many years ago. Before I was even born. A few years after the war."

"Perhaps you might recognize the woman in the painting?"

I held up my phone to show Gianpaolo the picture. He squinted as he looked at it. "I don't…" He looked a little harder and then called out, "*Mamma, vieni qui.*"

"*Perché?*" a woman shouted from behind the door.

Gianpaolo sighed. "*Vieni qui e lo capirai, mamma.*"

We heard a heavier sigh come from behind the door, and a woman who looked to be in her late 60s came through the door holding a stack of papers and wildly gesturing with her arms at what I'm assuming was her son. "*Che cosa c'è, Gianpaolo?*"

When she saw us, she stopped. "*Ah, mi scusi,*" she said, placing the papers on the counter and turning in our direction.

"*Parla inglese, per favore,*" Gianpaolo said, before turning to us. "This is my mother, Amelia."

"I apologize for my outburst to my son," Amelia said with a thick accent. "How may I assist?"

Maggie spoke up. "We were hoping you could tell us about this artwork that we found in the botanical garden in Lacusara." She held the picture on the phone up for Amelia to see.

Amelia gasped. "*Mamma mia!*"

Maggie laughed. A cliché, yes, but it really is a common phrase in Italian.

"Yes, a surprise," I said.

"No, I mean, this image, it looks much like the pictures of my mother when she was younger," Amelia said. "Here, let me show you."

Amelia went over to one of the walls behind the bar, which was filled with pictures of people and grapes and grapes and people. She pulled off a picture that appeared to be an old family portrait—one of those formal black-and-white photos with a good dozen family members sitting sternly for the camera. All except one young woman in the back row on the left. She had long black hair and an infectious smile that stood out.

"*Ecco*," Amelia said, pointing to the smiling woman. "This is my mother, Sofia. And this…" she said, pointing at an older man in the middle looking most stern, "is her father, my grandfather. He is the one who brought the festival to town. It was a big deal for an international festival to come to a small wine region like ours. He spent the rest of his life talking about the year the wine world came to Bonvini. Of course, as the hometown of the great artist Paolo Luciano, they thought the event should have something to serve as a… *come se dice… manifesto…*"

"A poster, perhaps?" I said.

"Poster?" Amelia said, shrugging her shoulder. "*Si o no,* it was a very large painting on a wood carving the size of a door used at the entrance to the festival. *Mia madre* was at the nearby *accademia d'arte* and found a young artist to paint it. There were paper versions printed from the original painting, of course, but they all disintegrated or disappeared. I never knew where the original ended up. Where did you say you found this?"

"It's in the botanical garden in Lacusara, behind the gate and covered by some vines," I said. "Not easy to find, I will say, but we happened upon it."

Amelia looked at the picture on my phone again. "It was obvious from the look on the face of *mia madre* that the artist who painted the picture was quite taken with her. We always heard that although my grandfather liked the painting, he did not like what it represented. That may be why he did not keep any copies."

"I showed the artwork to an art historian from my university," Maggie said, "and he found the painting to be quite accomplished and said that this woman was much loved."

"She was. Is, actually. She is much loved, if…"

Maggie's eyes lit up. "Wait, she's still alive?"

"Yes, although she does not live here with us in Bonvini. She in fact does not have much to do with us anymore."

"We try," Gianpaolo said, shrugging his shoulders. Amelia shot him a look.

"She is almost 90 and said it was too difficult to live here in the country after my father died. For the past 10 years, she has stayed in the city…."

Gianpaolo stood behind Amelia, shaking his head back and forth and mouthing, "They don't speak."

Amelia turned to look at him, but he feigned innocence with a smile. Maggie and I tried not to laugh.

"Even when I was young, she spent a lot of time with my grandfather on my mother's side at his palazzo in Lacusara," said Amelia. "*Papà* worked here at the winery, and she would disappear for days at a time to the palazzo."

"Taking care of her grandfather," Gianpaolo offered.

Amelia brushed his comment aside with her hands. "*Mamma* likes the city where she can promenade with her dog along with everyone else," Amelia said.

"What did I tell you about the dogs, Emilio?" Maggie whispered to me before saying to them, "I am quite fascinated with the painting. Do you think your grandmother would speak with us?"

"You might have more luck than we do," Amelia said, sighing. "I will warn you that her English may not be the best, but you can't miss her in town. She has a routine: mornings in the botanical garden and then after siesta to the cafe near the park. She has a very old dog with a great deal of long hair. I always tell her that he looks like a mop."

Maggie got a big smile on her face that led me to believe she already knew exactly who they were talking about. I did as well.

♡ ♥ ♡

The energy on the bus on the trip back to Lacusara could not have been more different than what we'd had in the morning. Quite electric, with everyone comparing adventures and souvenirs. The rugby players were covered in dirt and smelled of beer. The Paolo Luciano enthusiasts were chatting about some frescos they'd found in his childhood home. Those who had taken the original tour seemed ecstatic they'd gotten in more sights and time for craft shopping than they might have with a larger (and therefore slower moving) group. And our group, well, they were full of good wine and a great bike ride through the countryside and had the pink cheeks to show for it. Even Hilda, the dour tour director, had a semblance of a smile as she sat in front near the driver Vincenzo.

 We arrived back at the hotel right on schedule at 4:30 p.m. While they all had a chance for a short rest, I headed to the bar to set everything up for the 5 p.m. cocktail hour. At 6 p.m., the UC Berkeley folks had a scheduled lecture from a curator at the archeological museum who would preview their tour of the museum and the basilica the following day. Typically, a few people wanted to bring a cocktail to the lectures, so I liked to be ready. We also had a group of Brits in-house. Like the Aussies, they tended to grab a pre-dinner beer, so I was glad to see Matteo had seen my note and made sure the Peroni were on ice. By 8 p.m. or so, the groups would head off to whatever dinner plans they had—the UC Berkeley group had a free evening—and I could start closing things down and head home.

After a day spent riding a bike through the countryside and wine tasting, I will admit I felt rather tired. Then I saw Maggie hanging out in the lobby after the others left for the lecture, and my energy returned. I gave a small wave, and she walked over. *Kaplump. Yes, heart, I can feel you beating there.*

"What a day, huh?" Maggie said.

"Amazing," I said, then asked. "Aperol Spritz?"

Maggie smiled. Oh, how I liked her smile. "*Si. Per favore, Emilio.*"

"*Molto bene*," I said.

As I made her drink she said, "I'm kind of hungry. Are you hungry?"

I smiled. "Actually, I am. The snacks they put out at the wineries were great but not particularly substantial."

"No, they were not."

"You know," I said, "I know a great place for dinner close by, if you don't mind waiting until I close down the bar. We could have dinner around 8:30?"

"I do not mind waiting at all," Maggie said with a smile. "I'll meet you here at 8:30."

Just like that, my energy returned, and at 8:45, Maggie and I found ourselves at Da Ugo, a small cave-like restaurant with maybe a dozen tables run by a friend of mine from Florence. It was close to the hotel and, more importantly, somewhere I had never brought Bianca or any of the other women I'd dated since arriving in Lacusara.

"I love this," Maggie said as we sat down at a small table in the back.

"It's great, isn't it? Ugo used to be the executive chef at a five-star hotel in Florence. Hated it. Came home and opened this place as a way to do what he loves on his own terms."

"Impressive. And a great story," Maggie said, turning and looking me straight in the eyes. "You bring all your girls here?"

Man, those green eyes of hers pierced right into my soul. Part of me wanted to run away from the scrutiny while the other…

"You are the first. Scout's honor," I said, crossing my heart and holding up two fingers.

"You were a Boy Scout?"

"Brooklyn Troop #183," I said with a smile.

"Okay…"

Soon a short, ebullient man wearing a chef's apron came up to the table. "*Emi—perchè non…*" Ugo said.

"*Inglese, Ugo, per favore.*" I tilted my head to the right, and he saw Maggie sitting next to me.

"*Signorina*. I did not see you. Hello, my name is Ugo."

"Pleased to meet you," Maggie said.

"I was just going to ask why Emilio was not sitting at the bar by himself as is his usual manner, but now I see it is because he has a most attractive friend."

Maggie smiled as Ugo kissed the back of her hand. "I made some fresh gnocchi today," he said. "Perhaps with a nice *insalata e vino rosso*?"

♡ *Emilio* ♡

I raised my eyebrows and looked to Maggie for approval, and she said, "That sounds wonderful."

"*Grazie mille,* Ugo," I said, and he hustled away. Soon, we had a carafe of local wine and a basket of homemade focaccia in front of us.

"So…" Maggie started before taking a bite of the bread and moaning in happiness. "Oh my god. I might need a moment."

"Take your time," I said, allowing her some time to enjoy the bread. "It's amazing, right?"

"Beyond amazing."

"So…" I started this time. "Tell me, Maggie…"

"Are we back to Maggie now? At the winery, you called me Margherita."

"Well, yes, that would be your name in Italian."
She smiled. "I like it."

"I'm glad. So… tell me, *bella* Margherita, what is your story? How is it you are here on your own?"

"Well, I am attending the trip in an official capacity."

"That is not what I'm asking."

Maggie laughed. "I know," she said, looking at me more seriously. *Kaplump.* "You want the short version? I fell in love. Hard. Got my heart broken. Figured out who I was and how love worked. Created a paramilitary relationship counseling service that was then used against me to fall in love again. The first guy returned. I decided neither was the right guy."

"Not a tale you hear very often," I said, laughing.

Maggie smiled. "I suppose not. And you?"

"Me?" I said, thinking. "Well, I did the year abroad in Florence. Stayed for graduate school. Married. Fast. Young. Divorced. Fast. Young. Came here to get away from it all."

"You win for the shortest version."

"Don't mean to. I just never know how to talk about it, except to say I felt like a huge failure."

"You don't have to … talk about it. I get it."

"Thanks. I appreciate that." And I did. Nice to feel understood.

We clinked glasses as the food arrived. Maggie took a bite and gave another moan in pleasure. "Oh my god."

"Yeah, Ugo's the real deal."

"I love that he doesn't want to be famous."

"Being famous is overrated."

"Ain't that the truth," Maggie said. "Not that I am, but I did write a book that sometimes brings me more notice than I would like on campus."

I laughed. "Was it about—what did Monique call it—your superpower?"

"Superpowers are overrated."

I laughed again. "Speaking of your superpower, thank you for introducing me to the crazy dog thing here in Lacusara. I had not noticed that not only does seemingly everyone in town have a dog but that they are all different breeds."

"Hard to imagine how you couldn't see it. I mean, hello?" Maggie said, waving at what I'm assuming was a promenade o' dogs going on outside the door.

"I've been trying my best not to notice anything, I suppose."

"Why do you think that is?"

"I don't know. I was burned. And I do deal with the public, you know, every single day."

"I hear you…"

"I mean, the truth is… I hate to say it, but… well… in general, there are days when I feel that people kind of suck."

I tried to lessen the negativity in my statement by offering a small smile and adding, "Personal company excepted, of course." But instead of being shocked or appalled, Maggie's eyes widened. Then she did the most surprising thing: She pulled me in for a kiss.

Chapter Ten
MAGGIE

Yeah, I kissed him. I couldn't help it. I mean, the man got it. Oh my god. He GOT IT. People suck! Yes. They really, really suck, even if, okay, some of the people I recently met (him included) didn't *totally* suck. The fact he understood—really understood—my view of the world took the little pheromones I had been holding at bay and released them in a wave that surprised even me. So, I grabbed his face, and I kissed him. And he kissed me back. And it was good. Oh my god. It was reeeeeal good. The type of kiss that brings a tingling that starts at the top of your hairline and radiates down to your pinky toes. Wow.

But now what? Whatever the "now what" was, I didn't want it happening there in front of everybody in Ugo's restaurant, even if we were tucked in a secluded corner. Thank god Emilio felt the same way and quickly signaled to the bartender. *"Il conto, per favore, Luca."*

The bartender nodded and soon we were walking. Holding hands and walking. And, again, while I knew it was just the pheromones talking and whatever was about to happen would just be a fling, I felt… just… wow. It was totally out of character for me to take the hand of a man I'd known for maybe 72 hours and follow him home, but it somehow felt right. Well, I started to follow him home. We had only gone a few blocks before I stopped in my tracks.

"So, uh, Emilio."

"*Si?*"

Just the sound of his voice and my insides started tingling a little more. "I'm assuming we are headed to your place…"

He turned to look at me. "Is this wrong?" he asked, his soft brown eyes looking deep into mine.

"It is the opposite of wrong," I managed to croak, "but it occurs to me that we both have to be at the hotel really early in the morning, you to make the *doppio macchiato* that makes life worth living…" I gave him a soft kiss on the cheek for that. "And me to do my scheduled meet-and-greet of the group at breakfast before they head out to the archeological sites."

We thought for a moment and then said, "The hotel" at the same time.

I laughed. "Yes. But stealthily."

Emilio raised his eyebrows on that one. "Stealthily."

Oh god, man, stop doing that, or I'm going to jump your bones right here in the street, I thought. We took a left turn down a ridiculously charming cobblestoned street and headed back to the hotel. We snuck up the back stairs like teenagers with sleeping parents in the next room. Hell, most of the group I was traveling with could have been my parents (or even grandparents), so it felt appropriate.

We got up to my room. I slipped the key card in, and we stepped inside. I was glad now that my room was on the far end of the hotel so no one could see and/or hear us, because—and I'm going to be honest here—the minute we got into the room I jumped, and I mean JUMPED, into his arms. We both fell pretty loudly onto the bed and started laughing. I didn't care. I had to keep kissing him and hugging him and... (Yes, I dot dot dotted you here. I am a lady, after all), or my body was going to burst into flames.

Neither of us burst into flames, but the connection was goooood. Soon, we were snuggled together in a tight ball on the bed, and for the first time in a long time, I felt content. My usually frenetic brain quieted as Emilio softly kissed the back of my neck. I grasped his hands and held those gorgeous fingers. It occurred to me that even if this was just a fling, I would be okay. The joy I was feeling at this particular moment was something I would always feel. I then realized that "joy" perfectly described the look on the face of the woman in the painting. Is this what she was feeling? All I knew was that whatever this was with Emilio and however it ended, I was in the midst of an amazing moment of connection with another human being—a human being who did not, after all, suck (not in the figurative sense anyway). I laughed at the machinations my brain was making.

Then I heard Emilio say: "Why are you laughing?"

I thought for a moment. "I just really like Italy," I said.

He laughed and kissed the back of my neck again. "And Italy really likes you."

♡ ♥ ♡

When I awoke the next morning, Emilio was gone. I looked at the clock: 7:30. Shit. I needed to get downstairs. I threw on some clothes and headed down to the tables set aside for the Cal group in the breakfast room.

"Your *doppio macchiato, signorina*," I heard over my left shoulder as I entered the room.

I turned and Emilio was handing me the concoction that—along with the man—provided such happy thoughts. The word "joy" popped back in my head, and I again wondered if that's what the woman in the painting was feeling.

"*Grazie mille, Emilio*," I said.

"*Prego, Margherita*," he said with a slight raise of the eyebrows.

Even though using the Italian version of my name made me sound like a pizza, it also kind of excited me. And here it was only 8 a.m. I briefly wondered if Monique could show me the closet she and Mike used for their trysts as Emilio went back to making more coffee and espresso drinks for the hordes of tourists milling about the breakfast buffet.

I joined one of the tables assigned to our group and took a sip of my *macchiato*. Heaven. As my brain continued to wake up, I noticed the talk at the table centered on all the fun they'd had the day before—well, except for our difficult child, Clark, who sullenly read a museum brochure while the rest of the group discussed that day's agenda. Most were staying with the archeological museum and tour, but a few decided they would prefer to stay at the hotel or enjoy more of the town. A couple intrepid spirits indicated they wanted to return to the rugby academy.

I then noticed that Hilda or Monique or someone had placed cards on the tables. I picked one up. It listed activity choices for the following day, which would be our trip to Verniciara. I realized I hadn't seen Monique since I'd left the bus the day before, so I went into the lobby to look for her. I found her tapping furiously into her phone in the lobby with a furrow in her brow starting to look a little like the one Hilda always had.

"*Buon giorno,* Monique," I said, in my chipperest tone (almost made me barf).

"Maggie," Monique said in a very unchipper tone.

"Everything okay?"

"Yes, no. Well, it will be." She looked up at me. "Hey, are you going on the archeological tour today?"

"I actually wanted to talk to you about that. I was kind of hoping you or Hilda or Wilcox or whoever's in charge now wouldn't need me. I'd like to look more into that artwork in the botanical garden."

"That's fine. And I'm not in charge. Hilda and Wilcox are still the leaders," Monique said, although her tone said that maybe she wasn't quite sure about that. (Uh oh, talk about messy!) "I just can't find Hilda at the moment, and Vincenzo is here with the coach to take everyone to the archeological museum. Could you do me a favor and get a head count from the breakfast crew of those going? I know some are choosing to just hang out here today."

"Happy to," I said, walking back into the room where they served the breakfast buffet.

"And while you are there, grab the cards they've filled out with their chosen activities for tomorrow," Monique called.

When I walked back into the breakfast room, I noted that tables one and two had new groups (Scandinavians where the Brits had been and Canadians in the place of the Koreans) before walking over to tables three through five where our group had congregated. I asked each table who was going on the archeological tour. The majority raised their hands. Again, a few were choosing not to go: a mix of the older/slower folks who decided the tour involved too much walking and the two in the rugby group. Mike had told them that they were welcome anytime that week and that Fabrizio would be picking them up to head back to Bonvini for that day's scrimmage and language lesson. Language lesson should really be in quotes because from what I could see that meant hanging out and drinking beers with Fabrizio and his friends. I suppose, to be fair, that is one of the best ways to learn a language.

I went back out to the lobby and found Monique with Hilda. I handed Monique the cards and told them they could expect 18 on the bus and that all were headed up to their rooms and would be outside ready to get on at 8:30 as planned. Then I returned to the breakfast room to, you know, actually eat a little breakfast. I sat with my plate as almost everybody else headed out. The Thompsons sat two tables over contentedly looking out the window at the view.

"Life goals, am I right?" I heard over my shoulder. I turned to find Emilio.

"Monique and I both said the same thing when we first met them."

"You're not going on the archeological tour?"

"I am not. I've been given a hall pass as I would rather go back to the botanical garden and learn more about that painting—and quite possibly the woman behind it."

"Would you like some company?"

"You have time?"

"My morning shift ends at 11, and I walk home that way every day."

"It's a plan, then. How about I meet you outside the front of the hotel at 11?"

"I'd like that," said Emilio. "Would you like another *doppio macchiato*?"

The way he said it was so sexy I almost grabbed him and pulled him in for a kiss, decorum be damned. But, no, I played it cool.

"Desperately," I said with a smile.

After my second macchiato and a quick shower, I decided on a whim to put on my blue dress that looked similar to the one in the painting, even if I felt a little self-conscious. I headed down to the lobby, passed through the front door, and started walking in the direction of town. As planned, I soon found Emilio by my side.

"You look lovely today, Margherita," he said.

"Still sounds like a pizza."

"A pizza named for a queen."

"Is that right?"

"*Certamente,*" Emilio said, looking at me more closely. "That dress is a similar color to the one from the painting, yes?"

I could feel my cheeks flush a bit. "Very similar," I said. "This will probably sound weird, but I thought since I had the dress, I should take a picture of me wearing it next to the painting. My friend Kathy back home will never believe me otherwise."

Emilio smiled, and we continued walking into town. Once we got a couple blocks away from the hotel, he took my hand in his. Wow, that felt good. I turned and smiled and got one in return. What was it about this man that made me feel so damn good, so comfortable? Whatever it was, I planned to enjoy the hell out of it until I had to return to the real world.

We walked through the gate that led into the botanical garden. I noticed Emilio do a quick scan—I'm guessing to make sure his ex Bianca wasn't there. I did a scan myself. There weren't any tour groups in the garden at that moment. We walked over to the wall behind the gate and pulled back the thick foliage. There she was: the woman in the painting, wearing her now-very-faded blue dress and somehow not-at-all-faded joy-filled smile.

"Do you mind?" I asked, handing Emilio my iPhone and clicking the camera app.

"It would be my honor." He took the phone and snapped a few photos. He then asked me to put my hand over my heart like the woman in the picture. It felt cheesy as hell, but I did it and laughed as he snapped away.

"Would you like to take a photo, you know, with me?" I asked.

"Also to send to your friend?"

I could feel my cheeks flushing. "Maybe."

"I would be honored," Emilio said. He walked closer, again performing the incredibly sexy motion of pushing the hair out of his eyes with his fingers. He then turned, took me in his arms, and held the phone up above us.

"*All'Italia,*" I said, smiling.

Emilio laughed. "*All'Italia* indeed."

He snapped a few quick photos, then put the phone down, turned, pulled me closer, and planted another kiss on me. My lips started tingling at the touch.

"Oh," I said.

"*Si, é vero,*" he said as we kept kissing. And it was good. As great as our night together in my room was—and it was great—there was something incredibly special about kissing this man in this beautiful garden in front of a painting that intrigued me so much. It created a light in me that I hadn't felt in a long time. I kept returning to the joy radiating from the smile in the painting. The artist captured the emotion so perfectly that it made me want to know the story behind it even more.

Then, over Emilio's shoulder, I sensed movement. I looked and saw her: the well-dressed woman with the furry footstool, a.k.a. the old Pekinese dog.

"Emilio," I said, not wanting my lips to leave his as I said it.

"Yes," he said, doing the same.

"I think that's her…"

Emilio pulled back reluctantly (I hoped; no, I knew) and looked behind him. I pointed toward the elegant older woman holding her furball of a dog as she strolled through the garden.

"You really think Signora Vitarelli is the woman in the painting?"

"I do. Her daughter described that Pekinese to a T, don't you think?"

"You and those dogs. What did you call it?"

"A Pekinese."

He laughed and pointed at the mass of fur the woman was carrying. "And you're sure that's a dog?"

I laughed as well. "When I saw the woman at the cafe on the square my first day here, I thought she brought her own furry footstool everywhere she went. Her daughter called it a mop. But no, that is a dog. And yes, it is a Pekinese. At some point, I'm going to have to introduce you to the Westminster Dog Show so you can learn all the names. Anyway, since we know that everybody in this town has a different breed of dog and that one is the designated Pekinese…"

"*Si, si… va bene,*" Emilio said. "I see what you mean. I know Signora Vitarelli but not well. She can be a little shy, so let's wait until she gets settled on her usual bench. Then we will walk by, and I can introduce you, and you can ask about the picture. In the meantime…" And then he planted another kiss on me. Oh my god, the man could kiss. Then he took those sexy fingers and touched them to mine, and the feeling was accentuated. I may even have sighed (the good kind), which made him smile. We pulled apart, and Emilio looked across the botanical garden with a quizzical look.

"She did not stop," he said.

"I'm sorry?"

"Signora Vitarelli always stops and sits on that bench over there," Emilio said, pointing to a wall down on the left. "When I walk home for my lunch and siesta…"

Lunch and siesta, I thought. *How civilized.*

"…after my morning shift at the hotel, I always stop and say hello to her."

"Where do you think she went?"

"I do not know. This is a mystery." Emilio shrugged.

"I saw her at the cafe my first afternoon here," I said. "She might be there."

We walked through the botanical garden toward town and did a tour of the cafes and the dog park but did not find Signora Vitarelli.

"It is a little early for an *aperitivo*," Emilio said. "She may have another appointment in town or at home."

"True," I said.

"Until we solve that mystery, perhaps the two of us can go and have some lunch."

"Lunch and a siesta?" I asked.

"Oh yes. I believe lunch and a siesta are definitely in order," Emilio said. "It is how we do things in Italy, after all."

"Have I told you how much I am enjoying Italy or, as you say, *Italia*?"

"*Si. All'Italia.*"

"*All'Italia,*" I replied in my best attempt to mimic an Italian accent.

He took my hand in his, and we walked through the botanical garden toward his home. "*Vieni qui.* Let's go home."

I knew it was probably a translation thing that made him say "home" instead of "my place" or "my house," but in what was a very odd turn of events with someone I had just met days earlier, it felt appropriate. I mean, I knew it was just a fling. I knew it wasn't home. I knew we would only be spending time together for another few days. But I realized that I would be okay. For the first time in my life, I was living in the moment. I was, not unlike the woman in the painting, happy.

Chapter Eleven
MONIQUE

Adding flexibility to the tour schedule went spectacularly well. The new itinerary made a lot of people happy, with Clark our only problem child. What a pain in the posterior. Always moody, always complaining. Why in the hell did he come on this trip? Luckily, he seemed somewhat placated by the fact we still offered the original schedule, just not for everyone, so I did my best to ignore him.

On the flip side, the changes seemed to reinvigorate both Hilda and Professor Wilcox. They were no longer at each other's throats when they got off the bus at the end of our trip to Bonvini. Hilda even chatted with Vincenzo while Wilcox helped the Thompsons off the bus as they continued discussing their viewing of the Luciano frescos. The rest of the group also wore smiles on their faces—and in the case of the rugby players, a few grass stains—as they chatted about their day's adventures. Not only did their countenances differ from the day before, but they also presented a marked contrast with the other groups staying at the hotel, many of whom shared a dull pallor that can come from following a guide blindly from place to place.

The success of our day in Bonvini led Hilda and me to look over the schedule to find additional days where we could offer the same kind of variety. The following day, everyone was scheduled to tour the archeological museum and the basilica. There, a strict schedule had to be adhered to in order to get the group in and out in a timely manner, so it wasn't feasible there. But the day after that we had the planned excursion to the town of Verniciara, the home of the art academy established by Paolo Luciano. That day, we could add optional classes at the academy to the basic walking tour of the town. After that, we had a free day back in Lacusara, where we could set up activities such as an Italian lesson at a cafe, a tasting seminar at a local wine shop, and a more in-depth tour of the botanical garden. We even added the option of taking the train into Turin or Milan.

Then there were the two members of the group who indicated they would be interested in skipping all of the above and continuing the rugby drills with Mike and post-game "language lessons" (a.k.a. beers) with Fabrizio. Rugby. I will come clean here and tell you that it doesn't matter how many times I watched the sport or had Mike elucidate it. To me, it still looked like a bunch of ridiculous running about and slamming into other people while throwing an oddly shaped ball here and there. I could see no apparent form or function to the exercise. It was not unlike American football (another rather unfathomable endeavor, in my opinion), albeit played without all the helmets and padding, which made it even crazier. But Mike adored the sport. Saw each game as a microcosm of life. A smattering of the tour group members ended up loving it as well—a tall, thin woman I hadn't talked to yet and a bookish man who'd mentioned he was a NASA scientist. Neither were what I considered "rugby types"—i.e., built like my Mike—which piqued my curiosity a bit as to the sport's attraction.

While those two chose to spend their days crashing into other intrepid souls, a few opted out of any planned activities—mostly the older couples, including the Thompsons, whose mobility (especially hers) wasn't great. Free from the societal constraints of following the tour, they instead chose to spend some of their days sitting on the chairs on their balcony, holding hands with big smiles on their faces. Good for them. Others preferred strolling into town to sit at a cafe and people-watch—or dog-watch. Once Maggie mentioned all the dogs in town, I couldn't stop seeing them either and became just as curious as to the story behind the phenomenon, especially as the relationship between Italians and their dogs out in the country could not have been more dissimilar. In the countryside outside Bonvini, I often saw dogs left outside and neglected, but Maggie was right that here in the city they were quite pampered and, in this town at least, consisted of a variety of purebreds.

As for Maggie, she could not stop seeing Emilio. It was pretty obvious they had started *Bienvenuto in l'Italia*-ing. And, yes, I know I'm not one to talk, me of the equipment-room and luggage-closet trysts with Mike. I'm glad Maggie had a chance to experience a modicum of happiness. Although I missed spending time with my friend, I couldn't remember the last time I had seen her smile the way she did with Emilio. As long as she continued to recognize it as a dalliance, I didn't see any harm. The two of them also appeared to be involved in a caper involving a painting they had discovered in the botanical garden. I had no idea of the particulars, but again, Maggie's apparent joy made me happy.

With Hilda traveling with the group to the archaeological museum and Maggie spending the day with Emilio (wearing, I have to say, a very attractive blue dress), a great deal of the planning had fallen on my plate. I recognized I had brought it all on myself as I found myself in the lobby of the hotel arranging the following days' activities. Although I felt we had the blessing of Beverly back in the alumni travel office at UC Berkeley to tinker with the schedule—she did say she wanted to add more flexibility (right?)—and had managed to bring Hilda on board, I knew we needed to fly under the radar of Scholarly Travel Adventures. To achieve this, I ensured we still visited all the sites promised in the original brochure and kept to the overall schedule, even if not everyone saw every site. Most importantly, we stayed within the designated budget with any extra activities paid for directly by the participants. I thus avoided adding any new vendors that might submit invoices they wouldn't recognize. The feat I was attempting was to provide everyone the trip they wanted with no complaints to the tour operator or the university's alumni travel department.

Once the group headed off on the bus to the museum, and I saw Maggie headed out of the hotel, I mapped out all the activities and sent confirmation emails to the various entities. Then the hotel became very quiet. Too quiet. I have never done well with total silence. Luckily, my reverie was broken by the appearance of Fabrizio at the entrance to the hotel.

"Fabrizio, what are you doing here?"

"I'm picking up Rose and Alan for today's workout at the rugby field."

"Oh, that's right. I forgot they weren't going to see the archeological sites."

"No, they choose to continue with the lessons about the rugby." Fabrizio smiled. "They have been having a most enjoyable time. As have we. It is too bad they are not staying longer as Bonvini could use them in our game next weekend against Ottiglio."

Soon, I saw Rose and Alan walking down the stairs into the lobby, both wearing traditional rugby-striped shirts branded with the Bonvini Rugby Academy logo.

"Nice to see you, Professor DeVellier," Rose said.

"Please, call me Monique," I said. "Fabrizio tells me you two are playing rugby again today instead of going sightseeing with your spouses."

"Definitely. I haven't had this much fun in a long time," said Rose.

"I haven't either," Alan said, adjusting the bandage he'd placed over his nose. "It probably won't surprise you to learn my mother would never let me play contact sports as a child. Who knew what I was missing?! Would you like to join us today, Monique?"

I thought about it. I had completed all the preparations for the next few days, so why not? "You know, I think I might," I said, already smiling at the thought of another visit to the equipment room with Mike as I packed up my bag.

I climbed into the backseat of Fabrizio's ridiculously small Fiat with Rose. To avoid watching Fabrizio's driving (which was frenetic, to say the least), I turned to Rose and attempted to make small talk.

"We haven't really had a chance to chat," I said. "I hope you are having a good time."

"Amazing time," Rose said. "Much better than I thought I would, in fact."

"How so?"

Rose thought for a moment. "Well, when my husband said he wanted to come on this trip, I wasn't sure. I spent a lot of time in Italy during my graduate studies, but he had never been. He found this trip in his alumni newsletter, and the dates worked well with our schedules, which can be difficult to match up, so I agreed."

"Makes sense."

"I'm not saying I wouldn't have been fine with the original itinerary. Neither of us have the time to organize a trip like this, and it's very well put together. Gary's enjoying the original itinerary immensely. On the flip side, I have never been a fan of overly structured travel, and I've seen the churches—believe me, I've *seen all the churches*. So when you offered the opportunity to try something a little different for a few hours each day, I was ecstatic." Rose paused. "In my everyday life, I don't get a lot of time to just play, you know?"

"Oh? What is it you do?"

Rose hesitated. "I'm a priest."

I turned and gave her a look. The athletic woman sitting next to me in the workout clothes was a far cry from the black-collared old men with Irish brogues I associated with the title of priest.

"I hope you don't mind if I say that you don't look like a priest."

Rose laughed. "I'm an Episcopalian priest. As it happens, we come in all shapes and sizes."

"Sorry," I said. "I don't mean to stereotypically categorize."

"Not at all. It's a strong stereotype to break, but you can see why I hesitate to tell people. It changes the way they look at me," she said, smiling.

"I get it," I said. "I've often had that issue myself."

"Surface impressions don't always match up with what's inside."

"No, they do not." I paused for a moment. "So… rugby. You like it?"

"I do!" Rose said. "It's not something I'd ever tried. At home in Malibu, I play beach volleyball, and I played other sports in college but never rugby. It's awesome."

Awesome, huh? Before I could query her further, we had reached the athletic facility. I contorted myself out of the Fiat's backseat and saw Mike in the distance with the dozen or so players signed up for that week's clinics. I waved. As he walked in our direction, his smile lit up his face.

"Hey, baby, what a great surprise," Mike said, pulling me into a hug. "Two days in a row!"

"Too quiet at the hotel," I said.

"We do not have that problem here."

"No, you do not," I said, still astonished that even the most banal conversation with the man could ignite such a fervor in me. Mike took my hand and turned to Fabrizio.

♡ Monique ♡

"Fabrizio, why don't you get these two started with some stretches and warm-up drills? I'm going to go and grab some extra knee pads."

I laughed. See, I knew my husband was smart enough to use something like knee pads as an excuse!

"*Certamente*, Coach Mike," Fabrizio said with a smile. I'm not saying it was a good excuse, but Mike at least tried, right? "*Andiamo,* Rose and Alan. Come with me."

They headed over to the field, and I followed Mike back into the sports facility offices and our favorite equipment room with the foam mats placed strategically on the floor.

"I missed you, baby," Mike said, pulling me in behind him.

"It's been less than 24 hours," I said, laughing and wrapping myself around him once we got inside.

"I know," Mike said, locking the door and starting to unbutton my clothes with a multi-tasking ability that was quite impressive. "I'm still a little curious about this surprise visit, though. Things okay at the hotel?"

"Yes, but…"

"But what?" he asked, continuing his impressive multitasking abilities and using his even-more-impressive leg strength to lower me down to the mat.

"I guess…" I managed to eke out, doing some multitasking of my own. "I guess, well, everybody seems to be getting their ideal Italy trip."

"And…"

"Uh… well… oh… yes, well, except me."

"And what is it you would like, my love?"

"Well, obviously this."

"You always have this. No matter where we are. You know that."

"I know. And I appreciate it…" I said as a certain point was accessed that made it increasingly hard to form words. "Oh so appreciate it…"

At that point, mono-tasking took over, and soon I heard the *Benvenuto in l'Italia!* we had grown to know and love. We took a moment to lie on the mat holding each other.

"I have to get back out there," Mike said, kissing me on the top of my head.

"I know," I said, words returning.

"But I want you to be happy before I do that."

"I am happy."

"I know, but what you were saying before… How can we add to *your* Italy experience?"

I thought about my conversation with Rose in the car. About her ability to subjugate preconceived stereotypes through the playing of sports. Not to mention the glee that Alan, the NASA scientist, had expressed. As an intellectual, the dichotomy intrigued me.

"What do you think about me joining you all on the rugby field?" I finally said.

Mike got a huge grin on his face. "I thought you'd never ask," he said. "How about today? We're just doing some light training."

"I'm not properly dressed."

Mike looked around the room filled with shorts, t-shirts, sweats, and, yes, knee pads, in addition to other gear. "I think we can find you some proper equipment."

And that's how I ended up joining the rugby scrum out on the pitch. (Look at me all jaunty with the lingo, even if I'm sure it's not particularly accurate.) This week's group consisted of adults in the early stages of learning the game, so it was easy to stick me in. After some rudimentary lessons, Mike created two teams, and we participated in running and passing drills before playing a scrimmage (I believe that's the appropriate moniker) against each other. As I passed the ball—still peculiar looking, in my opinion—back and forth with my teammates, I started to glean an understanding into the nature of sports and their popularity all over the world. The involved synchronicity and group dynamics created an endorphin rush I usually only felt, well, let's just say in the equipment room with Mike.

And then… and then… I found myself running toward the goalpost carrying the ball, my teammates doing their best to protect me on either side. As I ran, I pondered the feelings it provoked. Of course, before my analysis could get too esoteric, I realized the opposing teammates were attempting to thwart my progress. I tapped into what I can only describe as a primal urge to move the opposing team's players the hell away from me. I zigged in one direction. When they followed, I zagged back, managing to take the legs out from under the two players closest to me. Oh my, it felt good to see them fall into a heap on the ground.

"You're okay, right?" I called as I heard Mike laughing on the sideline.

"You don't ask if people are okay when you thump 'em! Just thump 'em!" Mike called back. I looked back and smiled at him. I felt a modicum of complete and total satisfaction before encountering the sensation of someone taking my legs out from underneath me and grabbing the ball. Within an instant, I found myself sitting on my butt on the grass field. Huh. Interesting.

After a few hours of this, we were all exhausted and caked in grass and dirt (and maybe a little blood, but I'm not sure whose). To gather sustenance, we walked over to the bar closest to the field. As I walked in, I saw Bruno, whose family ran both the cafe in the Bonvini town square and this bar near the athletic field, and noted his surprise that I was not in my usual pristine attire. We ordered food and beers and practiced our Italian with Fabrizio. It was… well, it was quite pleasurable. I mean, I wasn't happy about landing on my butt, but the high that came from dropping the others on theirs kind of made up for it.

I pondered the camaraderie participating in a group sport had engendered. I knew studies had been done on the concept of collective effervescence in the sports realm but had never really paid them much attention. It's not that I actively disliked sports or group endeavors. I

Monique

had just never been one of those people for whom they played a large part in my life. And now, suddenly, I found myself not only deeply ingrained in creating an innovative travel experience for a group of UC Berkeley alumni but also partaking in a sports experience. And enjoying myself, to boot. I suppose, as my new friend Rose (the priest who'd had a part in tackling me on the field, I should point out) had said, it was still possible for people—including me—to be surprised.

Chapter Twelve
EMILIO

"Say it again," Maggie said, quietly lying in my arms as the sunlight filtered through the window in my apartment, and the sounds of the town coming back to life could be heard right outside. "C'mon…" she said. "Say it."

I did: "People suck."

She gave me a kiss. "And again."

"People … suck."

Maggie sighed. "They really, really do."

We both started laughing. At first, it was just a small laugh. But somehow the idea that our low viewpoint of the human race drew us together—coupled with the giddiness of the laughter itself—grew until we were laughing so hard that I felt tears coming out of my eyes.

Once that subsided, we fell back into the same position. Maggie looked around the room.

"I like your place."

"*Grazie.*"

"It's well organized."

"I pride myself on my organizational skills," I said (somewhat facetiously).

"Kudos to that." Maggie paused for a second. "It feels like a sanctuary."

"It definitely has been."

"That's how I think of my place in Berkeley as well. An escape from the horribleness of the human race."

"Well, they're not all horrible," I said, looking at her.

Maggie glanced up at me. "I suppose they aren't."

Maggie then turned her gaze over to my desk, at the computer and the stacks of papers and DVDs that had been shoved in the corner and not looked at in months.

"What's the scoop with all of that?"

"Nothing."

"Doesn't look like nothing to me. What's your story, Emilio…" She looked up at me. "What is your last name, anyway?"

"Montanari," I said, watching her roll the name around silently. "And I told you the story."

"You gave me the crib notes version. Let's start with this: What were you studying when you came to Italy?"

"Film."

"Interesting. Like you want to make movies?"

"Like I study their impact as a sociological force."

Maggie laughed. "People think I study movies, too. They're disappointed to learn I'm the type of communications professor that studies group dynamics instead."

"Are you disappointed that I studied movies instead of making them?"

"On the contrary, I'm intrigued. But I'm more intrigued as to why you stopped and how you ended up at the Hotel Botanico in Lacusara, lovely as it may be." She looked at me and smiled.

God, I loved that smile. I wondered if she knew how close it was to the smile in the painting. I felt my heart clench in a good way but also in a kind of scary way.

Breathe, Emilio. Just breathe.

"Intrigued like you are about the picture?" I said, desperately attempting to change the subject. I then noted the time on the clock on the wall. "Speaking of which, we should probably leave soon if we are going to try to catch Signora Vitarelli at Pietro's cafe."

"You're deflecting again, but I'll allow it."

"You'll allow it?"

"This time."

"This time?"

"This one time," she said, pulling me in for a kiss. "But you're going to have to pay."

"Oh, I am, am I?" I said through lips still attached to hers. "In Aperol Spritzes?"

"No."

"In *doppi macchiati*?"

"Definitely not," she said, pulling me closer.

"Oh…" I said, doing the same.

♡ Emilio ♡

♡ ♥ ♡

Later that afternoon, we walked back to town through the botanical garden, looking to make sure Signora Vitarelli wasn't sitting on her bench. We took a peek at the painting, which was still there under the vines. Of course, it was. It had been there for more than half a century. We then headed over to Pietro's cafe in the town square. We sat at one of the tables with the best view of the nearby dog park. I had to admit it felt a little odd. Sitting in a cafe and leisurely having an *aperitivo* was not something I had done in a very long time. Everybody else—both locals and tourists—did it on a daily basis, but I pretty much just worked my shifts at the hotel and retreated to my apartment. My sanctuary, as Maggie called it.

"So where, exactly, are you in your film studies?" Maggie asked after we ordered our spritzes, although on my suggestion, we mixed it up and ordered Campari Spritzes instead of the Aperol version.

"I'm sorry?"

"Before you tabled your film studies, where were you? Bachelors? Masters? Ph.D.? ABD?"

"ABD?" I asked, knowing exactly what she meant.

"All But Dissertation. Don't they use that here?"

"They do. I was—what do you keep calling it?—deflecting."

Maggie turned to look at me. She took my hand and said, "You don't have to answer if you don't want to."

"No, it's fine," I said. "I was ABD, but my break from the dissertation has been so long there's a chance I may never finish it."

"What's your topic?"

"It's pretty esoteric and maybe a little woo-woo."

Maggie laughed. "More woo-woo than trying to make love logical by creating a paramilitary relationship counseling service?"

I looked at her and laughed. "Maybe not."

"Then let's have it."

"As I mentioned, I'm combining disciplines—not just film theory but sociology and psychology—in looking at the power of art, film in particular, to transport us."

"Kind of like the smile on the woman's face."

"Yes!" I was amazed she understood what I meant and realized why that painting had always been so mesmerizing for me. "In art, we find experiences that transport us, remove us from the everyday. With film, the distillation of images and sound can provide a transcendent experience."

"Transcendent is definitely a woo-woo word," Maggie said with a grin.

"I warned you," I said, laughing, but I really wanted her to understand and found myself getting more excited as I did. "From the early days with films like *A Trip to the Moon* by George Melies in 1901—which while silent would have had musical accompaniment—the combining of moving pictures with sound has provided viewers with a sense of wonder or awe. As you may know, there's been a lot of recent research on the science of awe…"

"The psychology department at UC Berkeley has been involved in that," Maggie said.

"Yes, yes it has!"

"I've consulted with them here and there on projects."

"Oh, right! I didn't really put it together. I was actually in Berkeley doing some research with them a few years ago."

"We might have walked right past each other," Maggie said, grinning.

"I wish we had met," I said, taking her hand.

"Me, too. But I don't want to interrupt," Maggie said. "Go on."

"Well, there's been a lot of study on how music shifts our neurophysiology, breaking down the boundaries we feel between ourselves and the outer world. I'm looking at how adding visual images multiplies that. Moving pictures and sound coming together provide a sensory window into both the vast wonders of the world and smaller moments like gestures of simple human kindness—you know, like the end of Frank Capra's *It's a Wonderful Life*—those moments that create…"

"Goosebumps."

"Yes, exactly!" *Oh my god, I can't believe she gets it!* "For me, that first goosebumps experience happened when I saw the original *Star Wars*. My uncle loved the film, and when I was ten years old, he insisted my brother and I see it for the first time on the big screen. We took the subway into Manhattan and went to a special screening at Lincoln Center. The coalescing of the elements of the film together with the love from the crowd created… how do I say this…"

Maggie nodded. "A formative experience."

"Yes! That's the academic coming out of you, but yes, absolutely formative and related to the Kantian exploration of the symbiotic nature of viewer and artist."

"Now who sounds like an academic?" Maggie said, laughing. I have to admit I was kind of surprised how awakened I felt and wondered if that meant it was time to get back to the dissertation. It had been pretty difficult to study awe and wonder when I myself felt nothing beyond a tepid "meh."

"But I get it," Maggie continued.

"My particular work focuses on the effect this coalescing of elements has on children," I said. "That first glimpse we have of awe or wonder or mystery in a movie similar to the one I had watching *Star Wars*. Those moments when you first learn there can be such a pure distillation of beauty in this world…" I said. I almost added "like you" but decided it was too cheesy, even for me.

Maggie again gave me a smile not unlike the one on the woman in the painting. Then I spotted the woman herself: Signora Vitarelli. She was walking out of the park, very slowly because her old dog was walking alongside her. "I think I see the furry footstool you mentioned."

Maggie laughed. "Her daughter called the poor thing a mop."

"Both quite apt descriptions."

We watched as Signora Vitarelli continued across the square and into Pietro's cafe. In a wonderful bit of luck, she took a seat at a table right next to ours. Maggie and I turned toward each other so she wouldn't notice we were watching and waited until she was situated. The staff, obviously well acquainted with her, brought out a bowl of water for her dog along with a glass of red wine and a plate of olives, nuts, cheeses, and salami.

Signora Vitarelli smiled as she looked out on the square. She took a sip of her drink and glanced over in our direction. I saw a glimmer of recognition, so I tipped my glass, and she did hers as well.

"Signora Vitarelli," I said, "it is so nice to see you." I spoke in English, hoping she would understand that Maggie did not speak Italian.

It took a moment for Signora Vitarelli to realize she knew me from our meetings in the garden.

"Oh, Emilio," she said. "It is nice to see you as well." I was happy to hear that her English was, in fact, impeccable, if heavily accented. Her head swiveled over to look at Maggie.

"May I introduce my friend, Margherita?" I said, again using the Italian version of Maggie's name.

Signora Vitarelli nodded. "It is very nice to meet you, Margherita. I have to say, I very much like your dress."

Maggie looked down and then over at me. We'd both forgotten she was wearing the dress similar to the one in the painting, but it gave us a perfect opening.

"Thank you," Maggie said, nodding at me.

"Signora Vitarelli," I started, "we discovered a painting in the botanical garden with a woman wearing a similar dress and thought you might be able to help us find out the story behind it."

"I don't know how I might be able to do that, Emilio."

"You spend more time in that garden than anybody," I said, deciding it best not to mention we had spoken to her daughter. "Do you mind if we show you a picture of the painting?"

"*Sì*. That would be fine."

I pulled out my iPhone and showed her the picture we had taken of the painting. I could swear I saw a very brief start and a slight smile at the sight of the picture.

"Where did you find this?" Signora Vitarelli asked.

"It's on the wall behind the West Gate covered by some vines."

"Oh," Signora Vitarelli said. Then she paused before speaking again. "Unfortunately, I do not think I can help you. I do not know the painting or the woman portrayed in it."

♡ Emilio ♡

    With that, she dropped some money on her table, picked up her dog, the furry footstool, and walked out of the cafe.

Chapter Thirteen
MAGGIE

Emilio and I were both stunned that Signora Vitarelli walked away. Just walked away.

"What do we do now?" I asked. "Do we follow her?"

"We did tell her where we found the painting," Emilio said. "Do you think she's going to look for it, even though she said it wasn't her and that she didn't know the artist?"

I shrugged my shoulders, kind of frozen with not knowing the right move. I was also still reeling from the discussion of Emilio's work, which was so much more interesting than I'd ever imagined. Not only was the man handsome as all get-out, but he was smart and interesting and funny. Of course, I couldn't ponder the romantic ramifications because, even if she didn't walk all that quickly, Signora Vitarelli began to move out of our sights.

I started to pull some euros out, but Emilio held me back. "No, no, I got this." He put the money on the table to pay for our drinks, and we both got up.

"We're not following her," I said, "as much as, you know…"

"Strolling through town…"

"We have always enjoyed the botanical garden…"

"One of our favorite places, is it not?"

I clasped his hand as I marveled again at how in sync I felt with him. We started walking in the direction of Signora Vitarelli, who had not gotten far when we spotted her on a small street filled with shops. We slowed down to a stroll so we could continue to follow unobtrusively. Every once in a while, Signora Vitarelli would stop and look back, and we would jump inside a shop or even grab a quick kiss. I felt like a spy. Well, I did until one of our kisses went a little longer. Before I knew it, I felt a tap on my shoulder and found Signora Vitarelli standing right behind us. Some spy, right?

"Why is it you are taking the time to follow me?" Signora Vitarelli asked in the sweetest voice possible, furry footstool back at her feet.

"We just really want to know about the painting," I said. "The joy in the woman's face. It, well, it spoke to me, and I would like to know the story behind it."

Signora Vitarelli smiled. Not quite the smile in the painting but a smile nonetheless. She nodded and pointed at a large metal door embedded in the wall next to us.

"This is my home."

"Oh, oops!" We backed away quickly.

"*Scusi,* Signora Vitarelli," Emilio said.

"*Va bene,*" she said. "*Seguitemi.*"

"She says it's all fine, and we can come in," Emilio whispered to me.

"Are you sure?" I asked.

Signora Vitarelli smiled again and nodded. "Please join me."

We went in through the big black door, which led us into an interior courtyard filled with potted flowers as colorful as those at the botanical garden.

"These are gorgeous," I said.

Signora Vitarelli beamed. "Flowers. They have always been my passion. My late husband had the winery, and I had the garden that surrounded it. Now I have this garden, which is more something I can handle."

She then led us through a door on the other side of the courtyard. We walked up a few steps and were greeted by an enormous living room with high ceilings. The wall on the far side of the room featured immense windows offering a stunning view of the botanical garden. I could even see the corner of the botanical garden where the artwork remained hidden. If I wasn't mistaken, I thought I could even spy a corner of the painting through the vines.

"Oh my god, this is spectacular," I said. "If this was the view from my home, I might never leave."

"But then you would not be around the people," Signora Vitarelli said.

I wasn't sure if I should tell her my philosophy that people, you know, suck. In general, of course. I decided to sugarcoat it. "I... unfortunately, I have never had the best impression of people," I said.

Signora Vitarelli smiled. "And yet you like this one very much," she said, pointing to Emilio.

I looked at him and nodded. He nodded as well and said, "One of the things Margherita and I share is the impression that people, well, *come si dice* slang for 'suck' *in Italiano*?"

Signora Vitarelli laughed. It was a big laugh that lit up her face and had her old dog dancing around her feet.

"What did you say?" I whispered to Emilio.

"I asked how to say 'people suck' in Italian."

I laughed and looked at Signora Vitarelli. "Not all of them, of course."

"No, of course. Please. Sit. I will have Lucia bring us an *aperitivo* since we missed having ours at the cafe." Signora Vitarelli walked down a hallway, the furry footstool following shortly behind.

"So, this is a real Italian villa?" I asked.

"This is a real Italian *palazzo*," Emilio corrected.

"What is the difference?"

"The size," he said, pointing to the tall ceilings and general immensity of the space.

Right. Duh.

Soon, Signora Vitarelli came back carrying the furry footstool. A small middle-aged woman followed behind her carrying a platter filled with cheese, salami, and olives. Signora Vitarelli then pointed to the bottles of wine lining the bar in the corner.

"Emilio, would you do the honors and pour us a glass of wine? Why don't we taste the Barbera? It's from the family winery."

I looked at Emilio as he got up to open the wine and he nodded, so I said. "We happened to visit your family winery as part of our tour of the area. It's really quite lovely."

"It was my father's passion and then my husband's," Signora Vitarelli said without giving away much expression in her face. "Now my daughter and her son run it for the family."

"They are doing a wonderful job. It was our favorite of the wineries that we visited."

"How nice to hear."

She nodded appreciably as Emilio brought the wine glasses over to the table. I thought it might be a good time to broach the subject of the painting.

"You mention your love of flowers," I said. "Is that why your picture is in the garden?"

Signora Vitarelli looked at me, again giving away nothing in her face. "I did not say the painting was me."

"You did not, but it's hard to miss that smile, which I saw on your face just a moment ago when you laughed."

"And on your face when you look at Emilio."

I may have blushed at that one.

"Especially when you wear that dress," she continued. "It is similar to the one in the picture, no?"

I definitely blushed at that one. "Yes. I was struck by the fact that I happen to own a dress similar to the one in the picture. We took a photograph to send to a friend of mine back in California. It is part of the reason why I am so curious about the story behind it."

Signora Vitarelli thought for a moment. She still didn't come out and openly admit it was her but did say: "It was a long time ago. Before, well, everything."

"Everything?"

Signora Vitarelli gestured to the room around her. "My life," she said. "It was a part of my life and not a part of my life, if that makes sense."

I nodded.

"When I was very young, I was rather headstrong, and I loved art," she said. I saw a glimpse of the grin from the painting again as she spoke. "My parents sent me to the *accademia d'arte* in Verniciara. There, I met this wonderful artist. The opposite of my family, which could be a little conservative. When my father brought the international wine festival to the area, he was seeking someone to create an illustration to help bring more interest. I suggested this person. My father was not happy when I brought him the painting. Especially when he saw the smile that had been painted on my face. He knew it would take me away from the plans he had for me and the winery. He brought me home from the *accademia* soon after and never told me where he hung the original painting."

"You didn't keep in contact with the artist at all?"

"No," she said, but a little too quickly, I noticed.

Signora Vitarelli looked at the two of us. "It was a wonderful love that I had, and I wouldn't trade those moments for anything."

Emilio and I shared a glance. I suppose that could refer to us as much as her time at the academy.

"Then I married the man my father had picked out for me. He was a very kind man and very passionate about winemaking. I was passionate about my garden and our family." She paused and looked at the pictures on the mantle of the two of them and their extended family. "My husband died ten years ago…"

"I am so sorry," Emilio said.

"Is that why you prefer living here instead of at the winery?" I asked, deciding not to mention that I knew she didn't speak to her daughter.

Signora Vitarelli nodded. "We had a good life there, and now I have my life here in the city. This palazzo was my grandfather's on my mother's side. Now it is mine. I live here with *Mocho*," which she pronounced as "moh-ko."

"*Mocho*?" I asked, looking over at Emilio, who was trying not to laugh.

"It means 'mop' in Italian," he whispered as Signora Vitarelli pointed to the dog at her feet. I smiled. Ah, so, the furry footstool had a name—and now I knew why her daughter called him a mop.

Before we could ask any more questions, Signora Vitarelli's helper Lucia came into the room and spoke to her in a quick burst of Italian I couldn't keep up with.

"Speaking of Mocho, it is time for his dinner. He is a very old dog and has not been feeling well recently. It is important that he have his medication with his food. I hope you do not mind if we continue our conversation another time."

"Of course," Emilio said, standing and heading to the door.

"Do you mind if we visit you again, Signora Vitarelli?" I asked.

"It would not trouble me in the least if you did," Signora Vitarelli said, smiling that smile of hers. "And please call me Sofia."

Sofia gave my hand a warm shake and added, "Until then, I hope you continue to enjoy Italy."

Sofia glanced in Emilio's direction. I smiled and did the same. "I will do my best, Sofia. *Grazie mille.*"

♡ ♥ ♡

On the next day's excursion to Verniciara, the options Monique created for us included sitting in on various classes held at the art academy. Yes, the same academy where Sofia Vitarelli met and fell in love with her artist. I couldn't wait to check it out. Do a little digging, as they say. As we boarded the bus (again with the 8:30 a.m. start—ugh), I made sure to check in with the group to see how everyone was doing. Smiles all around except for Clark, who continued to sit by himself with a sour look on his face. I attempted to sit beside him to see if I could bring him out by asking how he chose to come on the trip, but I swear he growled at me as he pressed his face into his book. I mean, it was a low growl but a growl nonetheless. So I pretended to hear Monique calling me and moved to sit next to her instead.

The art academy compound was located in the center of Verniciara. Based on the description in the itinerary and my first impression after getting off the bus, Verniciara revolved around the art academy the way Berkeley revolved around the university, if with a much smaller footprint. After a quick walk through the town and a tour of the art academy facilities—where I looked in vain amid its historical artifacts for clues about the artist who painted the wine festival poster—we were given a few options. We could continue with a more extensive tour of the town and local galleries or audit a class at the academy, where we could choose sculpting, pottery, sketching, glass blowing, or something called "Awakening the Creative Spirit." That particular course sounded similar to some of the art therapy classes I had been told might be useful in my consulting work. Practical gal that I am, I decided to take that one.

Naturally, the effect was not at all practical. To begin with, the instructor was a hoot. Close to Professor Wilcox's age, he could not have been more different than him in countenance. Small and wiry, with an energy I envied, he wore a multi-colored smock covered in paint splotches over black pants and had us sit on stools in front of easels set up with white sheets of butcher paper.

"*Buonagiorno a tutti,*" he began, weaving among the easels. "I am Maestro Carta. Yes, like you say the 'paper' in *inglese*. Here we say '*carta*.' Today, we open our minds through the placement of the paint on the paper, *si*?"

We all nodded with what I hoped was a respectable amount of enthusiasm.

"And now," Maestro Carta continued, pointing to a series of acrylic paints set up on a table in the center of the room, "you should paint."

"I'm sorry," I asked. "What do you mean by paint?"

"Pick a color and paint."

"Paint what?"

"Whatever you would like. Perhaps a self-portrait or a scene representing your time here in Italy," Maestro Carta said before turning back to the whole class. "It is not important what you paint. Or how you paint. Or how it looks. Just paint."

"What do you mean it's not important how it looks?" I asked

"Do not think about aesthetics. Let it be messy," Carta said.

"I don't like messy," I mumbled.

"Then you must embrace it even more," Carta whispered in my ear before turning back to the class. "I do not want you to think. At all. I want you to feel. Paint the feeling of Italy. The feeling of yourself in Italy. Do not worry about following form or function or anything attached to the logical left brain. Awaken the right brain. That is the essence of awakening the creative spirit. *Va bene*?"

"*Va bene*," I mumbled, still not particularly sold on the concept.

"In this instance, the utilization of art," whispered Professor Wilcox, who happened to be at the easel next to mine, "involves a freeing up of the artist, in this case us. It also teaches us a form of therapy that we can use to help others. This kind of course is not intended as much for fine artists as for those who might want to use art as a therapeutic device."

"Wow, that's very insightful, Emory," I whispered to him, using his first name as it seemed appropriate in this instance.

"Didn't know I had it in me, did you?" Wilcox said with a wink.

"I think I knew you had it in you, but I am glad to see it emerging," I said (and meant).

"My late wife was a psychoanalyst who often used art and theater and other cultural rituals with her patients," he said with a rueful smile. "She helped me see that art isn't just to be lauded for its aesthetic or historic significance, but as an aid to revealing more of our true selves."

Revealing our true selves. Interesting, I thought.

"That's also why this particular class is one of the first classes they have art students take when they start here at the academy," Wilcox continued. "It was one of Paolo Luciano's edicts that even for fine artists, it is important to tap into the psyche, as it were, and not get locked into classic modes of aesthetic beauty."

"Thanks, Emory," I said and, again, really meant it. Here was another person showing a side of themselves I hadn't taken in at first. Was Italy the kryptonite to my superpower with identifying people's inherent traits? It made me wonder if I could get through to Clark somehow. But that was for another time.

I turned to the easel and tried to think of how to paint myself or my time in Italy. I started with how I felt being in Italy and the emotions that were coming out by being in such a wonderful (and messy) country and spending time with a most wonderful (and decidedly messy) man. As I painted a scene from our trip to the winery (not well, I might add), I realized when I painted myself that I had a smile on my face and then realized I knew exactly who painted the picture of Signora Vitarelli.

"Emory," I whispered, noting that he was painting the botanical garden. "There is someone I need you to meet."

Chapter Fourteen
EMILIO

Maggie came back from her day in Verniciara absolutely bursting. I could see it in her face when she charged through the front door of the hotel after the tour bus let out. She immediately came over to the bar.

"May I get you an Aperol Spritz?" I asked with a smile.

"How about the Campari version?" Maggie said with a little eyebrow raise.

"Coming right up."

As I turned to make the drink, Maggie leaned in and whispered, "I figured out who the artist was that created the painting in the botanical garden."

"You did? Who?" I asked.

"Not now," Maggie said. "Later. After Wilcox's lecture. Everyone has a free night and will be heading into town for dinner, so come up to my room when you're done here."

Maggie took the drink, looked around again, gave me a wink, and ran off, holding a large piece of rolled-up paper in her other hand. I smiled and mentally calculated just how long I would have to wait.

After my shift ended at 8 p.m., I slipped up the back steps and quietly knocked on the door to Maggie's room. I looked around to make sure no one was in the hall. Although I knew we weren't fooling anyone, I also thought it better to keep up appearances at least somewhat.

Maggie opened the door, also looking down the hall quickly as I entered. She then immediately pulled me into a kiss.

"I missed you today," she said.

"I missed you, too."

We went on like that for a bit until I finally managed to croak, "So, what did you learn?"

"Oh, right," Maggie said, excitedly. "Okay, so, today I took the class at the academy that they call 'Awakening the Creative Spirit.'"

"Awakening the what?"

"Essentially, it's an art therapy workshop designed to tap into that decidedly messy right brain of ours," Maggie said. I probably still looked a little confused, so she continued: "In other words, we painted."

"Ah. Very nice," I said.

"You say that before seeing what I created."

With that, Maggie unrolled a large piece of paper, revealing a painting that appeared to be a woman in a blue dress riding a bicycle amid rolling hills filled with grape vines. At least, I think that's what it was. Really, all I could see were splotches and squiggles. I didn't know what to say until Maggie helped me out.

"Don't worry. I know it's awful," Maggie said, laughing hysterically.

"Oh, thank god," I said. "I wasn't sure what to say…"

"The look on your face was priceless," she said. "I wish I had taken a picture."

"I'm relieved you didn't."

"We were told to embrace the messy and not worry about it being pretty."

"Well, you followed the rules to a T."

"Right? Can you believe it? I embraced the messy, Emilio. That's not something I *ever* do."

"The messy was definitely embraced," I said, laughing.

"That's huge for me," she said. "And, okay, so I am not an artist."

"Well, maybe not a painter," I said, looking at her beautiful smile and green eyes. "You do have other qualities…"

"Oh, I do?"

"Most definitely," I said, my hands tracing the curves in her face. "Your intellect, for one."

"My intellect, huh?"

"And your humor…"

Maggie laughed. "Do you know that no one has ever appreciated my sense of humor?" she said, putting her palm over mine and lacing our fingers together.

"I would call that a deficit in their personalities, not yours."

"You are a very perceptive man, Emilio."

"No one has ever appreciated my perceptiveness, Margherita."

"I would call that a deficit in their personalities, Emilio."

We again went on like that for a bit. This time Maggie broke the spell.

"Okay, okay. So, we have established that I am not a great artist. Sorry, painter."

"Established."

"But I did figure out something while in the class…"

"Beyond the embracing of the messy?"

"Yes, beyond that."

"And awakening the creative spirit."

"Oh, yes, the creative spirit was totally awakened. And here is what it helped me figure out: Signora Vitarelli is the artist."

"I'm sorry. What?"

"Sofia Vitarelli painted the wine festival poster. The one in the garden."

"Signora Vitarelli? But how?"

"Well, as you can see, our instructor suggested we paint self-portraits. As I painted mine… bad as it may be… I realized Sofia painted herself. For those few years at the art academy, she got to be herself. Got to love herself."

"But she mentioned meeting an artist."

"And the artist she met was *her*. You'll notice she never explicitly said that it was another person."

I thought back to Signora Vitarelli's comments. Maggie was right that she seemed intentionally vague about the artist she recommended to create the artwork for the festival.

"That's true."

"Sofia loved her father and the winery, but her time at the academy opened up a whole new world for her as an artist. That's the emotion that showed up in her face."

"The joy," I said, realizing Maggie was right about the look on Signora Vitarelli's face in the painting. Joy was also the essence I was seeking to access in my dissertation—and, if I was being honest, my life. "You mentioned that word before."

"YES! Joy!! That's it! Exactly. Absolute joy." Maggie's face lit up as she said it.

Kind of like how I feel when I'm with you, I thought. But I didn't say it. First, because it was (again) too cheesy. But also because just as I started to feel that joy, a different wave of emotion took over. A crushing wave that said this was all starting to be too much. The last thing in the world I wanted to do was hurt Maggie, but the feelings I had for her were starting to be coupled with the abject failure I felt when my marriage broke up. Shattered might be a better description. Shattered in a way that made me distrust every decision I had made since.

When Maggie turned back to look at her painting—her beautifully awful painting that only made me care for her more—I took some deep breaths. We only had four more days together, and I didn't want to ruin them with my fears. I could get through this. Thankfully, Maggie didn't seem to sense the turmoil in my brain. Or maybe she felt something similar and wanted to keep the focus elsewhere as well.

"The question I have is how the painting ended up in the garden in the first place," Maggie said.

"Do you think Sofia put it there? Waiting for someone to discover it?"

"I don't know. Maybe, although she seemed genuinely surprised to see it. Either way, I feel like it's time that it—or at least the artist—had a bigger audience, don't you?"

"Yes, I do."

"I have an idea how to make that happen. It involves Professor Wilcox. Are you in?"

"You know I am."

♡ ♥ ♡

The following day was listed as a free day on the Berkeley group's itinerary, and it coincided with my day off. After most of the group headed out, either on their own or on one of the optional activities Monique had arranged, Maggie and I planned to take Professor Wilcox to meet Signora Vitarelli in the botanical garden. At 10 a.m., Maggie and I met Wilcox outside the front door of the hotel, and the three of us started the walk over to the botanical garden.

"How are you this morning, Emory?" Maggie asked as we were walking.

"Of more good cheer than usual, I have to say," Wilcox said. He really did look more jovial than I remembered seeing him before.

After we walked through the walls encircling the botanical garden, we pulled back the door to the West Gate and brushed aside the foliage to get a better look at the painting.

"It really is quite remarkable, even if the elements have not been kind to it," Wilcox said, examining the piece more closely. "I'm surprised I never noticed it during my visits to the garden in previous years."

"It's pretty well hidden," Maggie pointed out.

"This is true."

I looked out across the garden and saw Signora Vitarelli sitting on her usual bench with Mocho lying on the ground in front of her, panting. As Wilcox continued his examination of the painting, Maggie and I went over to greet her.

"*Buongiorno,* Signora Vitarelli," I said. "As you can see, our friend is examining your painting. He is a professor of art history and quite interested to learn more about your technique."

"My technique?" Sofia asked, looking over at Maggie.

Maggie nodded, looking directly at her. "Your technique, Sofia. Would you mind speaking with him?"

Signora Vitarelli looked at Maggie for a long moment while I held my breath. She then said, "Emilio, would you mind?" Sofia held out one hand while picking up her dog with the other. I nodded and helped her up. We all began walking back to the West Gate, where we found Wilcox continuing to pull foliage back to reveal more of the painting. When I stepped in to help him, Wilcox turned to look at Signora Vitarelli.

Wilcox gave a little bow in her direction and said, "Signora, my name is Professor Emory Wilcox. I am very pleased to meet you. This is your painting?"

Sofia looked again at Maggie and then back at him. Finally, she nodded. "It is mine. From a very long time ago."

"And you have more?" Wilcox asked.

Sofia pondered the question for a moment and then gave another little nod. I looked at Maggie in surprise. She opened her eyes wide and grabbed my hand.

"Could we perhaps see these additional works?" Wilcox asked.

Sofia nodded again, and I squeezed Maggie's hand a little harder. Unfortunately, just at that moment, Bianca came walking through the entrance gates holding a red flag ahead of a group of about 20 tourists (Brits, if the pink faces and occasional glimpses of the Union Jack on their backpacks were any indication). She stopped and looked in our direction.

"Please take some time to enjoy the entrance area of the botanical garden," Bianca said to the group in her heavily accented English. "I will start the formal tour soon."

As the tourists spread out looking at the garden, Bianca turned her microphone off and quickly strode in our direction. My heart started pounding as I took a few steps away from Sofia and Emory, still holding Maggie's hand. I offered Bianca a small smile to hopefully ward off whatever was coming. But instead of walking up to me, she walked straight up to Maggie.

"He's going to leave you, you know," Bianca shouted at Maggie as she pointed at me. "That is what he does with all of us. Makes us think we are special and then moves on."

I froze in my steps, inwardly cringing at the thought of what might happen next. But Maggie stayed calm. She dropped my hand and walked closer to Bianca.

"Bianca," Maggie said, gently touching Bianca's arm, "I appreciate your concern." Maggie looked at me and then turned back to Bianca. "If it helps, I am only here for a short time, so it is me who will be doing the leaving." Bianca got a confused look on her face and tears started falling from her eyes.

"I… just… I…" Bianca started.

"Oh, sweetie, I am so sorry for your pain," Maggie continued. "I've been there. I know how it feels."

Instead of lashing out, Bianca pulled Maggie in for a hug, sobbing into her shoulder.

"*Grazie, mille grazie,*" I could hear her mumbling.

"It's okay," Maggie said, continuing to hold her. "You're going to be okay."

Maggie looked over at me and then nodded in the direction of Professor Wilcox and Signora Vitarelli before speaking softly to Bianca. Although I didn't want to leave Maggie and Bianca together and was dying to know what Maggie was telling Bianca, I got the message and walked over to them.

"Perhaps we could discuss your art somewhere else, Signora Vitarelli?" I suggested.

Sofia nodded. "Why don't we go to my home? As you know, it is very close by." She motioned toward the building just outside the garden walls that Maggie and I had visited earlier.

"Excellent idea," Wilcox said. "Would you like to help me with your dog, Signora?"

"That would be most appreciated."

Wilcox lifted Mocho the mop, a.k.a. the furry footstool, as he and Sofia started walking slowly toward the entrance to the botanical garden near her home. I followed them, occasionally looking back at Maggie. She looked to be finishing up with Bianca, so I waited a decent distance away. My god, this was messy. And I didn't think it was the messy Maggie's art teacher had instructed her to embrace. Or maybe it was. Who knows? I saw Maggie give Bianca another hug before walking in my direction. I then looked at Bianca. I offered her a little smile and mouthed, "I'm sorry." For the first time in a long time, instead of daggers, I got a melancholy smile and a nod. A step in the right direction, I suppose.

Bianca turned her microphone back on, picked up her flag, and rejoined the group of tourists. "Over here, as you can see, we have the white lilies that are the national flower of Italy…"

As the group followed her in the opposite direction through the garden, Maggie walked back to me and took my hand.

"Everything okay?" I asked.

"Fine. Bianca will be fine." Maggie gave my hand a little squeeze, took a deep breath, stepped back, and looked up at me. "Here's the thing, Emilio," she continued. "I am going home in three days. We both know that this is just a fling–a wonderful fling, but a fling nonetheless. I just want you to know that I will always love the time we had here together."

I wasn't sure how to feel about that. The words felt so final, for lack of a better word. I suppose I should have been happy that Maggie wasn't trying to make what we had into something serious. It's what I wanted, right? So why did I feel my heart starting to break just a little?

Chapter Fifteen
MAGGIE

I didn't mean that to come off as harsh as it did. I mean, I said I loved our time together. That was true. But it came off rather glibly, and by using the past tense, it felt like I was making it clear I didn't see him as anything beyond an Italian affair. My intent had been to assure him I wasn't another Bianca and that I would be okay. I mean, we always knew this was just a fling, right? If I had learned anything from watching people like Professor Wilcox and Signora Vitarelli, it was that you had to embrace joy when you had it and not worry about the future. That's what I was doing. Right?

"I just want you to know that we're cool," I said, trying hard as hell to make myself believe it as well.

I kissed Emilio's cheek and continued walking in the direction of Emory and Sofia. It wasn't hard to catch up—with neither of them particularly fast walkers—and we continued our slow stroll over to the palazzo. Emilio stayed just behind us. When we got to the entrance, I helped Sofia and Wilcox through the door that led to the courtyard. I then looked back at Emilio and said, "Are you coming?"

Emilio stood for a moment and then smiled. "Yes. Yes, I am."

I took his hand, although I noticed he held it a little more gingerly than before, and soon we found ourselves back inside Sofia's gorgeous home. We showed Wilcox the window overlooking the spot in the botanical garden where the painting rested behind the West Gate. We all stood there for a moment, taking in the beauty of the botanical garden and the spot where the painting had stayed hidden for all these years.

After a few moments, Sofia said she had something to show us. We followed her down a long hall to a back set of stairs. She flipped on a light that illuminated a door at the top of the stairs.

"Emilio, could you help me open the door above, *per favore*?"

"*Certamente*," Emilio said. He bounded up the stairs, took the handle of the large door at the top, and opened it inward.

"I have not been up on that floor in a very long time, so I hope you will excuse the mess," Sofia said as she and Emory slowly walked up the stairs while holding onto the railing. The stairs were pretty steep, so I stood at the bottom in case either of them slipped, but they made it to the top like troopers.

Once I followed them to the top of the stairs, what I discovered astounded me. Like the living area below, the room was huge and featured a gorgeous window overlooking the park. But instead of furniture, the room was filled with paintings. Dozens and dozens and dozens of paintings. Most of the paintings seemed to have as their subject the botanical garden. Through seasons and years and decades, all of nature's transformations depicted in painting after painting. I'm no art expert, but I thought they were amazing. I could tell that Professor Wilcox also found them—to use his word from earlier—compelling.

"When… when did you paint these?" Wilcox asked, as he moved from painting to painting with a glee I had never before seen in him.

"As I mentioned previously," Sofia said, looking at Emilio and me, "this was my grandfather's house on my mother's side. The Vitarelli winery was my father's family, but this was my mother's family's residence. My mother knew about my love of painting, so after Father brought me home from the *accademia* and forbid me to paint, she would send me here to visit my grandfather regularly. They set up this floor for me as an art studio. This continued even after I married. I enjoyed the time with my *nonno* and painting the flowers outside the window. I replicated much of what I painted through the flowers I planted in the garden at the winery and country villa."

In silence, we all stared at the paintings that surrounded us.

"I know they are not very exciting..." Sofia said.

"Are you kidding?" Emilio said. *"Sono fantastici. Meravigliosi."*

"Professor?" I asked Wilcox quietly.

"Please excuse my silence," Wilcox said. "It is because I am in awe of your work, signora." He turned to look directly at Sofia. "If you would allow me, I would like to help you catalog these paintings."

"Oh, *Professore*, I do not think that is a worthy use of your time," Sofia said.

"It is a most worthy use of my time," Wilcox said. "And I happen to have it–time, that is–in abundance."

Sofia smiled and nodded. The three of us then spent some time looking through all of her paintings. When Sofia went down to ask Lucia to bring us some lunch, I found a series that included a young girl I assumed to be Sofia's daughter Amelia. The paintings depicted a toddler walking through the garden with an older man who looked to be her grandfather. I took a picture of the paintings. When Sofia returned, I was still looking at them.

"Does your family know about all of this?" I asked. "We met your daughter and grandson a few days ago when we visited the Vitarelli Winery..."

"It's how we found you," Emilio offered.

"No. They do not," Sofia said. "And that is as it should be."

"But they should know about these..." I said, wondering if I should mention the estrangement her grandson mentioned. I didn't have to.

"We do not speak. We had a disagreement," said Sofia. "As I said, that was my old life."

"But..."

"*Basta*," Signora Vitarelli said sharply. "I do not wish to speak of my family anymore."

Ouch.

"We will, of course, respect your wishes, Signora Vitarelli," Emilio said, giving me a look that said I shouldn't push.

Fine. I backed off.

"If you do not mind," Sofia said, "I think that is enough of a visit for today."

Sofia then turned to Wilcox. "It would be fine for you to examine my paintings further at another time, Professor."

"It would be my honor," Wilcox said, giving her a little bow.

With that, we trooped (slowly) back down the stairs. Wilcox, Emilio, and I left the palazzo through the big metal door and stood on the cobblestone street just outside.

"Shall we get a drink?" Wilcox suggested. "Perhaps a spritz that Emilio does not have to create himself?"

Although Wilcox's tone was downright buoyant, I felt a little—no, a lot—dejected by all that had just occurred. Between the encounter with Bianca and Sofia's still bitter feelings toward her daughter, I wondered if people were just not capable of, oh, I don't know, joy or forgiveness. Did they really, as I had been saying all along, just suck?

I kept coming back to Sofia's smile from more than a half-century ago. Was that smile just a moment in time that was never to be repeated, like the images Emilio studied in his films? That just all felt so depressing, as did the thought that the magical days I was spending with Emilio were equally transitory. What was I going back to in Berkeley? A sterile apartment, teaching Introduction to Communication Studies, and dealing with assholes on tech boards—that's what.

These thoughts roiled in my head as I pondered Wilcox's invitation. I realized I didn't really want him or Emilio to see my turmoil, so instead of agreeing to a drink, I quickly put on my sunglasses.

"I hope you two don't mind if I decline to join you," I said. "There's something I… I forgot to do."

That was a lie, but it got me away. I gave the two of them a brief smile and tried to ignore their confused faces as I walked—no, ran—down the quaint cobblestone road past the shops and the cafe in the square and into the park with the romping dogs. I tried to catch my breath. I didn't know where I was going. Mostly, I was trying to lose the vision I carried of Emilio's confused face. I mean, this—fling, affair, whatever you wanted to call it—was almost over, right? There were only a few days left on the trip, and the next day we were scheduled to be away from the hotel for our cooking lesson out at the Vitarelli Villa.

As I continued walking through the dog park (mentally noting a schnauzer, terrier, and poodle—and was that Clark in the far corner petting an Irish Wolfhound?), I felt a buzz in my pocket and looked at my phone. Kathy. I looked at the time. 2 p.m.

"Buongiorno!" I heard her say in a tone too chipper for what had to be the middle of the night for her.

"Buongiorno?" I said in a not-at-all-chipper tone. "What are you doing up? What time is it there?"

"It's 5 a.m., and I'm in our laundry room in the basement," Kathy said, laughing. "It's the only time I get to myself in this house. Why do you sound so … troubled?"

"Oh, Kathy…" Where should I start, right? "Well, you did say I should have an adventure, right?"

"Uh oh. What happened?"

I sat down on a bench near a friendly Newfoundland the size of a couch and realized how much I missed being able to pour everything out to my old friend. So I did. Everything. About Monique and I deciding to War Council Hilda and Wilcox. About meeting Emilio and discovering the painting. About Sofia and Bianca and Amelia and the wineries and the paintings and the art academy… and my heart cracking open just a tiny bit before being pounded back into oblivion.

"Wow," said Kathy. "You've packed quite a bit into a week."

"And we have another two days to go before we leave."

Kathy thought for a moment. "Okay. Tell me this," she finally said. "How were you feeling about Emilio before all the stuff with Bianca and Sofia happened? How do you feel about *him*?"

I sighed. "Well, I mean, he's hot," I said, and we both laughed. "And sweet, and smart, and intuitive, and well, fun. Really, we've just had so much fun."

"So why are you running away?"

"I'm not running away, Kathy. I'm taking a perfectly healthy stroll through a park with a ridiculous array of dogs."

"Uh-huh."

As had become usual with us, I started to become a little frustrated with her. It's a lot easier when you're on the other side of the world and never dated as an adult. "We can't all have perfect relationships like you do, Kathy."

"Ours isn't perfect," she said quietly.

"What are you talking about? You and Brian have been together forever and have two perfect children and that just didn't happen to all of us…"

Before I could continue my diatribe, Kathy said, even more quietly, "Brian left me."

"I'm sorry. What?"

"He left me. For one of his fellows on the Alaska project."

"Fellow?"

"Not a guy, Maggie, although there's a part of me that thinks I might understand that a little better than another woman. At least she's age-appropriate and not some young co-ed."

Wow. I wasn't sure what to say. Kathy and Brian. Brian and Kathy. As boring as Brian was (and he was boring), they were a constant. Met in college and had been together ever since. I was always the one with the volatile love life, not her.

The only thing I could think of to say was, "I'm so, so … sorry. Wow." I laughed. Not a laugh of joy, one of those sardonic laughs you make when you don't want to cry. "Well, we're a couple of funsters, aren't we?"

"I know, right? How embarrassing to be running the War Council…"

"I thought it was the Love Council."

"No, this is war," Kathy said. Now that did make me laugh.

"I suppose you could always sic them—or me—on him," I said, still laughing. "I'm not laughing at you. Really. Just laughing at how ridiculous it all is."

Then she started laughing. "I know, right? I mean, the man has been making me nuts, but what the hell am I going to do now?"

"You're going to be the same amazing woman you have always been," I said.

"Thank you, Maggie," Kathy said. "I know I haven't been easy to be around lately."

"At least I now know why."

"But that doesn't mean you should keep running away. Enjoy this man who has brought you such joy."

Joy. So much power wrapped up in such a small word. "But…"

"But nothing. Enjoy. We should all take whatever happiness we're allotted in this world when we can. Speaking of which, where have Mike and Monique been in all of this?"

"Who the hell knows?" I said, realizing I was gesturing with my hands as I did. *Hey, look at me, I'm turning into a real Italian,* I thought. "They've mostly been down at the rugby field."

"Yeah, I know Mike is there, but what about Monique?"

"She's been playing rugby, too."

"I'm sorry. What?"

Chapter Sixteen
MONIQUE

All I could think about the day after I played rugby was just how sore I was. Every muscle in my body ached, and I still didn't know whose blood I'd gotten on my shirt, which I'd thrown in the corner of my room at the hotel. Not one of the words in that sentence was anything I ever thought I would utter. Muscle aching? Blood on the shirt? Thrown in the corner? What was happening to me?

I wasn't the only one acting out of character. I caught Wilcox smiling (smiling!) and Hilda flirting (flirting!) with Vincenzo (Vincenzo!). And what the hell was up with Maggie? I mean, I had barely seen her, and then I learned she took the "Awakening the Creative Spirit" class, of all things, on our trip to Verniciara. Maggie? The organizational perfectionist and most analytical left-brain-leaning person I'd ever known "awakening the creative spirit"? Add in the hanging out with Emilio, and it was all just so out of character for her.

I guess I had been distracted. Between my day spent playing rugby while the group visited the archeological museum and planning the activities for the following days, I was *spent*. In case no one has ever told you before, travel planning is hard work, and throwing an oddly shaped ball up and down a field is *exhausting*! And I wasn't even compensated. For any of it! But amid all my complaining, I realized I found both the travel organizing and the rugby to be interesting challenges, a nod to taking oneself out of one's comfort zone. It was not something I did very often, but I had read studies on the phenomenon. The truth is, I was enjoying myself.

On the travel side, I got a thrill every time I managed to find the perfect activity for the perfect person and saw them beam with joy. For instance, in Verniciara, we treated the Thompsons to a talk with an artist from the academy in a cafe close to where the bus dropped us off, while Rose, my new Episcopalian priest friend (more words I never thought I'd use), learned glass blowing with her husband.

Similar to the first day when we mixed things up, I could feel the difference in the atmosphere on the ride to and from the town. On the way out, the bus was quiet. Yes, it was morning, the espresso drinks hadn't kicked in, and we'd come off a few busy days. Nevertheless. Quiet. On the way back, everyone was abuzz. Why am I using that word? I don't use words like "abuzz." I don't. But I have to say it fits. Buzzing, they were. Some of them displayed what they had created or related what they had learned in a conversation with an artist or on the tour of the academy or larger town. It made my heart proud, even if (as I said) every other muscle in my body still hurt from my previous day playing rugby. Let's just say it didn't look likely that there would be any visits to the equipment room with Mike for a while. Of course, if Mike came to the hotel, we could probably make something happen… But I digress.

The following day was the free day listed on the original itinerary. Clark couldn't get mad at me for that one! I merely arranged an array of optional activities, including Italian lessons at a local cafe, a tasting seminar at a local wine shop, a more in-depth tour of the botanical garden, and train tickets for those who wanted to take a day trip to Turin or Milan. Everyone was on their own, although I sat in the lobby (still sore!) with Hilda to make sure they all knew where they were going and with whom. A few chose to spend the day at the hotel or wander into town on their own to shop or eat somewhere they hadn't. Both Hilda and the hotel's concierge offered suggestions, with me handling the calls and emails. I wasn't sure how that became the new protocol and was not entirely comfortable having all of the planning dropped in my lap, but it had produced the intended effect of loosening up Hilda.

On the drive to and from Verniciara, she even sat up with the bus driver Vincenzo instead of constantly having her head in her phone confirming the next event. The two of them used the microphone to regale the crowd with stories about the sights along the way. Wilcox also seemed happier, talking with the Thompsons about the artist they'd met. Only Clark still seemed subdued, sitting in the back by himself.

Now Maggie, she came back from Verniciara with a gleam in her eye and then spent the free day with Emilio. I saw the two of them leaving the hotel around mid-morning, wondering where they were going. Add the sparkle from the painting class to the smile Emilio brought to her face, and Maggie was a changed woman. *Good for her*, I again thought, while also worrying where it might lead.

Then, *then*, I saw Professor Wilcox joining Maggie and Emilio as they walked into town. What was that all about? While I pondered, Hilda suddenly turned to me and said, "So… I think Vincenzo and I are going to head out."

"I'm sorry. What?" I said, looking at the entrance to the hotel where I saw our bus driver Vincenzo standing just outside. He gave me a nod and a wave. I turned back to Hilda.

"We're going to leave," she said. "I mean, it's not like you need me."

"Need you? You're supposed to be the one here at the tour desk today. I'm just helping you out, not taking over this trip."

"I thought about that, and I don't think so," Hilda said.

"I'm sorry?"

"Well, since you kind of commandeered this whole trip, I think that means you are now in charge."

What? What? Commandeered? Where is this coming from? I wondered.

"It's not like they have that much to go anyway," Hilda said. "Tomorrow, they spend the day at the cooking class out at the villa, and then it's just the final dinner and starting to prepare to head home. All that has already been planned."

Before I could protest any further, Hilda said, "I think you've got this covered," and practically ran out the front door, where I saw her greet Vincenzo–VINCENZO!–with a big kiss (eww!). And that's the last I ever saw of either of them.

I'm pretty sure my mouth stood agape for a good 30 seconds after she ran out. What the hell? And what was I supposed to do about it? I couldn't call Beverly and tell her that my little experiment with the trip had caused the tour director to go AWOL, especially when I had one member of the group still not pleased with the changes I had been making.

"Professor DeVellier," I heard over my shoulder. *Oh, great, speak of the devil.*

"Clark," I said with as calm a demeanor as I could summon. "How may I help you today?"

"Well, as you know, this was the designated free day on the itinerary."

"Yes, yes, I realize that."

"Yet you have scheduled activities for some of the participants."

"Those that asked me to, yes."

"Uh-huh. Uh-huh." He squinted his eyes.

"Is there anything you would like me to schedule for you?"

"No. I believe that I will stay with what is stated in the original itinerary as 'enjoy Lacusara on your own'…"

"Sounds like a wonderful choice."

"While ignoring the fact that others were accorded extras that I was not."

"They, of course, paid for those extras. They are optional activities."

"And yet they were not mentioned in the itinerary."

"No. Because they are optional activities paid for separately by the participants."

"And yet they were not mentioned in the itinerary," he said, finally starting toward the front door.

I sighed and mustered my best fake smile. "You have a good day, Clark."

Now, I'm not telling you all of this to justify what happened at the villa. I'm really not. But I think you can see where my patience was headed.

♡ ♥ ♡

Our day out at the villa near Bonvini had been promoted as one of the trip's highlights: "Learn to make pasta and pizza in a traditional wine-country villa." Everybody wants to do that when they come to Italy, correct? An almost obligatory activity, it had been part of the itinerary for years. The tour operator scheduled the cooking class at the Vitarelli Villa, the bed-and-breakfast located near the Vitarelli Winery, which some of the group had visited on our trip to Bonvini. I confirmed everything would be ready at the villa the day before and enjoyed the beautiful drive out there with the new driver that the hotel thankfully found for us, Arturo. So far, so good.

Sore as I still was, when the bus passed the town of Bonvini on the way out to the villa, I looked longingly at the rugby field and the cottage I shared with Mike and told myself I would be back there soon. I had texted Mike to see if he wanted to join us for the meal at the villa. He said he would try to come during his lunch break, and I felt warm just thinking about being near the man after the rather annoying days I'd had, between Hilda deserting the trip and Clark a constant thorn in my side and having to handle everything on my own.

When we arrived at the Vitarelli Villa, I noted the building's faded-brick facade highlighted by grape vines and dotted with lavender and rosemary bushes. Kudos, Scholarly Travel Adventures. Perfect choice for the event. As everyone disembarked the bus, they were greeted by Teresa Vitarelli (whom Maggie identified as the daughter-in-law/wife of the mother/son duo who ran the nearby winery) and a server holding glasses of their wine. Teresa then escorted everyone out to the villa's expansive back patio, which overlooked hills filled with rows of grape vines. Impeccable. Once everyone had taken the requisite photos of the tableau, they took their seats at the tables they had set up for us. I noticed people naturally gravitating to the kindred spirits they'd found along the way: The Thompsons sat with Wilcox and the other Paolo Luciano fans; the rugby players, Rose and Alan, sat with their spouses; and those who had taken the wine tour sat together as well. I sat at a table in the back in case I needed to take a call.

The cooking class began with Teresa's mother (the authentic "*nonna*" they promised) teaching everybody how to make tortellini, first making the pasta dough and then curving it into the appropriate hat shapes. Her mother spoke no English so Teresa translated everything. She talked about the history of pasta in Italy and offered amusing facts, such as how her mother thought pasta cured everything—from broken limbs to giving birth. Teresa then asked if any of the group wished to try making the tortellini themselves. About a dozen donned aprons and gave it a go while the others watched from their tables. Everybody seemed to be having a great time, aided by the carafes of Vitarelli wine provided on the tables.

Then Teresa brought in Bruno (yes, in addition to running the cafe and the bar, Bruno made the best pizza in Bonvini) to show everyone how to make pizza in the brick pizza oven the villa had installed on their back patio. Yet again, part of the group chose to get up close to Bruno to watch his technique and ask questions while others simply enjoyed the lovely summer day out in the country. I started to relax as I watched everyone enjoying themselves.

When I say everyone enjoyed themselves, I mean everyone except, of course, Clark, who did not partake. Yet again, he sat off to the side by himself. I thought I'd seen Maggie sitting next to him when we first arrived, but when I looked again, she was nowhere to be found. Perhaps even she had tired of the man at this point in the trip. I would have felt sorry for the guy if I hadn't tired of him myself. Those thoughts were interrupted by a familiar arm curving around to hug me.

"Hey, baby."

"Michael," I said, turning. "And Fabrizio! I'm so glad you both made it. We are about to have some of Bruno's amazing pizza."

Mike and Fabrizio took the seats next to me. We all watched Bruno's expert hands create enough dough for a few pizzas. Bruno then asked in his broken English for suggestions on toppings for each. They chose an onion and mushroom, a pepperoni, and a medley of vegetables. All was going swimmingly with a conviviality in the air that brought smiles all around.

Then… then… as the pizzas were going into the oven, Clark walked—no, strode—up to the table and asked Bruno if he was going to be making a gluten-free version of the dough. Bruno looked confused.

"*Che cosa?*" Bruno asked.

"*Senza glutine?*" Teresa offered.

"*Mi dispiace,*" Bruno said. "*Senza glutine? Come se dice senza glutine?*"

Bruno looked at me and I wanted to curl up in a ball in shame. Instead, I left my seat and walked over to the group in an attempt to placate the situation.

"Clark, you never indicated you required gluten-free," I said. "I mean, I know Hilda isn't here to verify your records, but you haven't requested gluten-free anywhere else we've gone."

"Yes, I know," Clark said, turning to me with stone-cold eyes. "But I'm kind of feeling like I've had too much bread on this trip, so I am wondering if I could have an option without…"

I don't know what came over me. In my defense, we were so close to making it to the end of the trip without anything going egregiously (or more egregiously) wrong, and this little prick just *wouldn't stop*.

"You want, what, a wad of cheese wrapped around onions and pepperonis?" I said, realizing the pitch of my voice was rising and knowing that hormones (not that those are at all a sign of weakness, I would like to reiterate to my women's studies compatriots) might have been playing a role in the oversized reaction I had to his lunacy. "IN ITALY???"

"Yes, Professor DeVellier," Clark said. "I want what was promised to me. The brochure indicated that gluten-free alternatives would be offered when possible. Without Hilda here, who are you to say otherwise? Besides, you have been making exceptions for everyone else and…"

I could feel my anger rise. I suddenly flashed back to running down the field toward the goal carrying the rugby ball with all those pesky defenders trying to stop me. So when Clark made a move toward Bruno and the pizzas, I… well, I tackled him. Not really a tackle, I just took his legs out so he ended up on his butt the way I did on the rugby pitch (I'm phrasing that correctly, right?). I mean, how annoying was he? Like a little gnat in my head for *days*. Dealing with people like him, I could see why Hilda was the way she was and had a whole new appreciation for what both she and Wilcox put up with on these trips.

While my move to take the man down engendered an undying amount of respect from Fabrizio (who said *"Benessimo placcaggio!"*) and Mike (who may have even uttered "That's my Kiki!!"), it generated not a little drama within the group. While many of them might have wanted to do something similar, the decorum breached by a professor tackling an alumnus remained quite egregious.

♡ Monique ♡

When things calmed down, the question remained: How could we fix things and end the trip on a high note? The answer came from an unexpected place and, unfortunately, involved a bit of tragedy.

Chapter Seventeen
MAGGIE

Our trip to the Vitarelli Villa was the first time I had seen the whole group together in a couple days. I enjoyed seeing the change in everyone's outlook and took some time to check in with people and listen to the stories about their adventures in town the day before. Once we arrived at the villa, I pretended to be participating in events of the day—the cooking class on the beautiful outdoor deck of the Vitarelli Villa—before setting in motion the plan to reunite the Vitarelli family.

Emilio and I had concocted our plan the same day I had my little meltdown. After getting off the phone with Kathy, I realized I needed to speak with him. I took the chance that he and Wilcox had still gone for the drink Wilcox had suggested and went to check the cafes in the square. I walked back through the dog park and the parade o' dogs (Weimaraner, English sheepdog, Malamute) and, indeed, found the two of them sitting at Pietro's cafe—the same cafe where I spent my first afternoon in Italy and the same cafe where we first contacted Signora Vitarelli. It was incredible that the cafe had come to hold such meaning for me in such a short time. Emilio and Wilcox were deep in discussion with drinks a light shade of yellow in front of them.

"Hey there," I said when I made my way to their table.

"Felicitations, Maggie," Wilcox said with a smile on his face. A smile!

"And what are you drinking, gentlemen?" I asked.

"Emilio has introduced me to the pleasures of the Limoncello Spritz," Wilcox said.

"Limoncello Spritz?"

"Did you know that there is a panoply of spritzes, Maggie?" Wilcox asked. "Even one that utilizes elderflower liqueur. How brilliant is that?"

"Quite brilliant," I said.

"Now, as its name suggests, this one utilizes limoncello from the Amalfi Coast, along with the requisite Prosecco from Treviso and sparkling mineral water," Wilcox said, obviously enjoying his quite immensely. "Am I missing anything, Emilio?"

Emilio looked up at me with his warm eyes and smiled. "Some people garnish it with basil and/or mint."

"Basil and/or mint?" I said, my heart swelling as I looked at him.

"Yes. You can have basil or you can have mint or you can have them both." Emilio stood and held out his hand.

"I think I would like that," I said, putting my hand in his and sitting down. I continued to hold his hand, and for a brief moment, all was right again with the world.

"Hey," Wilcox said, breaking through our reverie. "Have you two ever noticed the disparate variety of canines taking up residence in this town?"

Emilio and I started to laugh. Wilcox turned to look at us, wondering I suppose what we thought was so funny about his question. We nodded that, yes, we had noticed the dogs. Then I saw Wilcox's eyes briefly take in the sight of our still-clasped hands. He smiled, looked into his now empty spritz glass, and said, "I hope you two do not mind if I take my leave and head back to the hotel."

"We can walk you back," I said, starting to rise, as did Emilio.

"No need," Wilcox said, standing. "I have been to this city many times and know the way to the hotel like the back of my hand." He looked down at us. "But thank you, both of you, for bringing an old man a modicum of joy today. It is quite amazing, you know, to find that even at this advanced age, I can still be astonished. Unexpected, it is. Most unexpected."

Wilcox smiled again and started tottering off toward the hotel.

"You think he will be okay?" Emilio asked.

"I do," I said. I took a beat. "How about us? We okay? Sorry for my little meltdown earlier."

Emilio took his hands—his beautiful hands with the long, elegant fingers—and cupped them around my face. "Never apologize, Maggie. I will never not be okay when it comes to you." He pulled back, paused, and took a deep breath.

"Here is what I have been thinking," Emilio continued. "I don't know if we are the luckiest people in the world because we met or the unluckiest because we have to part soon. All I know is that any love we can find in this world is to be embraced for the moments it brings, even if they are brief."

"That is beautiful," I said.

"And it's not even from a movie," Emilio said, laughing. "Can you believe it?"

And with that, I kissed him again. How could I not, am I right?

♡ ♥ ♡

The plan Emilio and I came up with later that night was that I would, as scheduled, go to the Vitarelli Villa with the group. Then I would sneak over to the winery to try to talk to Amelia and/or Gianpaolo (not unlike the basil and/or the mint, huh?). While I was doing that, Emilio would visit Signora Vitarelli on his midday break from the hotel. Perhaps we were sublimating our own feelings about my impending departure by trying to mend the rift in their family, but it felt like the right thing to do. I kept flashing back to the pain I saw in both Amelia and Sofia's faces when they talked about not speaking and couldn't go home without feeling I had tried to do something to help.

I soon learned others on the trip might need a little help as well. While the UC Berkeley group seemed to be oblivious that anything might be amiss, I got the distinct impression something was up with Monique. Not only that, but we had a new bus driver, Arturo—young and slight, he was pretty much the opposite of Vincenzo—and Hilda was nowhere to be found.

"Everything okay?" I asked, taking the seat next to hers on the bus.

"Like you care," she said sharply.

"I'm sorry. What?" I asked.

Monique turned and looked at me and sighed. "Sorry I snapped. I am not sure what's happening to me, Maggie."

"Talk to me. What's going on?"

"Well, for one, Hilda disappeared."

"I'm sorry. What?"

"She just took off. With Vincenzo. Like two little love birds."

I started laughing at the mental picture of two of the most oafish beings I'd ever met running off together.

"Hilda and Vincenzo? Egads, Monique, how in the world did you end up War Counciling the wrong people?!" I asked, still laughing.

"I have no idea!" Monique said, cracking a small smile herself before the worry lines returned. "It was most definitely not my intention, and it's left me with quite the clusterfuck."

Now I knew she was serious: Monique never used words like "clusterfuck" (me, yes; her, no). "How can I help?" I asked.

"Just help me make sure that this event at the villa goes off as planned. If we can get through today, we only have the final dinner tomorrow, and that's at the hotel so we're kind of home-free. No one at the university or the tour operator will be the wiser, and I can go back to my normal life."

"Then let's do just that."

Famous last words, huh? After we arrived at the villa, everyone took a seat on the outdoor deck for the cooking demonstrations. The setting was spectacular, but my thoughts were so focused on what I would be doing next that I didn't get to enjoy it as much as I would have liked. I sat at a table in the back near Clark since no one else seemed to want to sit near him. He didn't growl at me this time, but he also didn't engage, turning to stare at the cooking class with his back to me. Once everyone was seated and occupied with the pasta-making demonstration, I slipped away and walked across the road to the winery I had visited four days earlier. I found the lovely young tasting room manager, Stefania, and asked for Gianpaolo or Amelia.

Soon, Gianpaolo came out from the door behind the counter.

"*Buongiorno, Gianpaolo,*" I started.

"I know you," he said, trying to place exactly where he knew me before continuing. "You are the girl who found the painting of my *nonna.*"

"I am." I nodded.

"You made my *mamma* very upset."

"I'm sorry about that, but after we talked to you, we spoke to your grandmother, your *nonna*, and… well, I think you should know…" I started, and then realized that it's true a picture is worth a thousand words. I pulled out my phone and showed him the pictures I took of Signora Vitarelli's paintings of Amelia in the garden when she was a child.

"That looks like…"

"It's your mother, Amelia, and it was painted by your grandmother, Sofia. It was among dozens of paintings we found painted by your grandmother."

I could tell he didn't believe me. "Nonna Sofia painted this? Where did you find these paintings?"

"On the top floor of her palazzo."

He thought for a moment. "I don't think we have ever seen more than the one floor."

"Sofia has been hiding a lot. She's also the artist who painted that poster for the wine festival all those years ago."

"The picture you showed me of the woman who looks like her?"

"It is her and also painted by her. A self-portrait she painted while she was at the art academy. Her father didn't approve and made her return home. Her mother and her grandfather then set up an art studio at the palazzo for her."

"All that time she was painting? An artist? And we did not know?" He shook his head. He looked at the painting of his mother as a child. "My mother always felt that Nonna Sofia didn't love her. She and my grandfather were very close. They both loved making the wine, but my grandmother… not so much. She created the garden here but spent much time with her mother's father at the palazzo in Lacusara instead of here at the winery. When her husband—my *nonno*—died, she moved there permanently."

"Sofia obviously loves you and your mother deeply, but she also loved her art," I said. "You and your mother share a love of creating great wine. You must understand having that kind of passion for something."

He nodded.

"Then help me get the two of them back together," I said.

Gianpaolo paused for a moment. "Why is this so important to you?" he asked. Not an unreasonable question.

I thought for a moment. "There's nothing I hate more than seeing two people who don't speak even though they love each other," I said. "It's … messy. I hate messy."

Gianpaolo again hesitated but then smiled and nodded. "Okay."

I had a moment of elation that our plan was working. Then I received the text from Emilio.

Chapter Eighteen
EMILIO

By the time I walked into the botanical garden after my morning shift, I knew that Maggie had made progress with Sofia's grandson Gianpaolo. Although it was the same walk I had been doing for years, suddenly everything looked different. More vibrant somehow. As I passed the West Gate, I looked behind it to say hello to the woman in the painting and then found the woman herself sitting on her usual bench with her furry footstool at her feet—about 100 steps and 65 years away from the picture that had been hidden there on the wall all those years.

"Signora Vitarelli," I said, nodding in her direction, "do you mind if I join you?"

"That would be fine, Emilio. And, again, I ask that you call me Sofia."

"*Grazie*, Sofia."

I sat down and let the sounds of the garden surround us.

Before I could say anything, Sofia said, "I know I need to speak to my daughter again. She has been very angry with me for a very long time."

"You realize that Amelia did not know about your art, especially the pieces you painted of her?"

Sofia looked at me. "Do you think it was wrong of me to keep all that a secret?"

"It is not up to me to judge."

Sofia sighed. "For years, my art was something special I shared with my mother and my grandfather because my father did not approve. More than not approve: He said I should not be painting and that the winery was the only thing that mattered for the family. My husband knew my secret. He was supportive of me having my own passions even after he took over the winery from my father. And then my grandfather died. And then my mother died. And then my husband died. The only people who knew about that part of my life were gone, and my daughter always seemed unhappy that I didn't love the winery like she did. I was afraid she would not understand, so I hid. From my family. From feeling."

"Maybe it's time to stop hiding," I said, saying it as much for myself as for her.

"You don't think it is too late?"

"I know it is not too late," I said. I waited a small moment before saying: "My friend Maggie is in Bonvini talking to your family."

Sofia looked over at me with a smile—not just a smile, *that* smile. "Margherita, you mean. She is special, Emilio. To you. Don't let that one go."

I turned back to her, surprised. "That one?" I asked, laughing.

Sofia gave a little nod of her head and a shrug. "I may be old, but I am not blind."

Ah, life in a smallish town.

Just as I was texting Maggie that Sofia was amenable to meeting with Amelia, Mocho, who had been asleep at Sofia's feet, started wheezing. It sounded worse than usual. A lot worse. I turned and looked at Sofia with concern as tears started falling from her eyes.

"Mocho has not been well for some time now," she said. "He does not have long. This morning, his doctor told me that today is most likely our last day to enjoy the garden together."

My heart sank. "Oh my god, Sofia, I am so sorry," I said, quickly texting that information to Maggie.

"Like me, he is old," she said, shrugging. "Of course, Mocho is also blind."

I smiled at Sofia's attempt at humor even as she was saying goodbye to her furry companion, tears falling down her cheeks. I reached for her hand.

As Mocho's wheezing started to get worse, I asked, "Should we take him to your home?"

"No," she said. "This garden is Mocho's favorite place in the world. He would like to be here."

"Would you like me to pick him up for you?" I asked. Sofia nodded, and I picked Mocho up and held him on my lap as I sat beside her. Mocho had so much fur that I hadn't noticed how skinny he had become underneath it. He hardly weighed a feather, as they say, as he relaxed into my lap.

Sofia and I sat quietly in the botanical garden for some time, listening to the sounds of the birds and the wind through the trees along with Mocho's increasingly labored breathing. Then I noticed movement coming from the West Gate. I looked over and Maggie came walking through. I nodded at the dog in my arms and Sofia at my side. She nodded back and then looked back as Sofia's daughter, Amelia; grandson, Gianpaolo; his wife, Teresa; and their two daughters came walking through the gate behind her. They were followed shortly after by Monique, Mike, Fabrizio, Professor Wilcox, and indeed, the rest of the UC Berkeley tour group. I even noticed some of the regulars from the dog park with their furry companions following closely behind, along with Bianca, who gave me a sad smile and a nod.

"They insisted on paying their respects," Maggie said when she reached us. "All of them."

Amelia came running over and knelt down to give Sofia a hug.

"*Mi dispiace, mia bellissima bambina,*" Sofia said. "*Ti voglio bene.*"

"*Anche a me dispiace. Ti voglio bene, mamma,*" Amelia said, widening her embrace to include the dog. "*E Mocho.*"

Amelia felt the dog, heard his breaths, and looked up at her mother, crying. Amelia hugged her even harder. Gianpaolo came and hugged the two of them and the dog, and everybody else joined in. I somehow ended up in the middle of a massive Capra-esque hug of humanity that I didn't realize how much I needed myself until I felt the tears start to fall from my eyes. It wasn't the dog I was crying for, although I had to admit I would miss seeing the furry little fellow in the garden every day.

Then, a most unlikely voice came through the crowd.

"I know I am not always the best when it comes to people, but I am very good with animals. I run an animal sanctuary back in California and have been through this process with hundreds of animals," said Clark, who walked closer and made eye contact with Sofia. "Would you allow me to help you and your loved one in his final hours?"

Sofia nodded, and Clark made his way through the crowd of people. I stood, and he oh-so-gently picked Mocho out of my arms and laid him on Sofia's lap. He then sat on the ground in front of the bench and gestured to Amelia and her family to come and sit on either side of Sofia.

We all watched, mesmerized, as Clark started petting Mocho very gently. He then took Sofia's hand and had her do the same while she held Amelia's hand with the other.

"You have given Mocho a wonderful life," Clark said.

I looked over at Maggie in the throng of people. We both had tears streaming down our faces. Everybody did. Even the Rottweiler.

"All we can ask for in this life is to love and be loved the way the two of you have," Clark said. "It is time for Mocho to take his leave, but you will always carry him and that love in your hearts, as will the rest of us."

Sofia nodded, still gently petting Mocho. After a few moments, Mocho's wheezing started getting lighter and lighter until the sound stopped altogether. When that happened, there was a collective sense of sorrow but also an emotion that felt an awful lot like awe.

♡ ♥ ♡

MONIQUE

Who *was* that guy? I mean, what the fuck, right? Clark, the sullen asshole who was always late, criticized everything we did, and wanted gluten-free pizza in Italy, for god's sake. Suddenly, he's this soulful individual?

Clark was actually the one who insisted we all go. When Maggie came running back to the villa to say she had to get back to town after Emilio told her that Signora Vitarelli's dog was dying, Clark said that these types of passings could be loving or traumatic, and we had the capacity to make a difference. I immediately thought:

♡ Monique ♡

Where did this guy come from? Is this the real Clark emerging from within the alien shell he's been wearing all week?

Needless to say, after all the drama in the botanical garden, Clark and I reached a detente of sorts. He later told me that his mother gave him the trip to Italy after the death of his own beloved dog, a dog that served as the emotional center of his sanctuary, and that was why he'd been so cranky. I suppose it helped me understand his mood. We all have those days, don't we? (But a week of them? In a row? Really? Sorry, I digress.) Clark said he didn't realize quite how bad he'd been until I took his legs out from under him. If I had known that, I would have tackled him a week earlier.

The following night, the Cal group gathered at the hotel for the final dinner. The collective earnestness that Maggie diagnosed on the first night was still in evidence, but it had been magnified by a loosening of inhibitions and a bonding over adventures that led to a camaraderie that hadn't existed before. Cards were shared, plans were made, and the Thompsons sat off to the side still holding hands and smiling as they took it all in.

I suppose if my goal had been to give them all a trip to remember—an immersion in Italian life—I had succeeded. Still, when Mike joined us, I made sure to *"Benvenuto in l'Italia"* his brains out in the luggage closet off the lobby. Yes, I had a room upstairs at the hotel, but by that point, I wasn't capable of making it up the three flights before I had my way with him.

♡ ♥ ♡

MAGGIE

If Monique ever thought that she had been discreet when it came to her trysts with Mike in the hotel's luggage closet, that all went out the window on the night of the final dinner. When Mike walked through the front door of the hotel, she practically grabbed him by his collar and pulled him into the small room, wrapping her legs around him as she closed the door. Luckily, I think I was the only one who saw it.

Emilio and I might have had a similarly entangled final night, but we at least had the good form to make it up to my room at the hotel first. Dealing with death and reunions and all the drama of the past few days brought out all the emotions. No holding back anymore.

But first, at the final dinner, I checked in with everyone. For the first time, Clark mingled with the group. It took a week—punctuated by a beloved pet's death and a smackdown by Monique—but he finally loosened up and was embraced by the others, which in turn made him less annoying. It caused me to realize that people can be capable of change in certain types of situations. I would have thought to study the phenomenon in more depth, but as I mentioned, I was headed upstairs with Emilio.

♡ ♥ ♡

EMILIO

My final night with Maggie was, in a word, magical. If all that we had just experienced taught us anything, it was that love and life were to be embraced whenever and wherever they could be found. Maggie and I acknowledged our appreciation of that fact and decided not to worry about what life may or may not bring in the future.

The next morning, I was up early to make sure everyone in the UC Berkeley group got their espresso drinks before they boarded the bus for the airport. I kissed Maggie goodbye and waved as she got on the bus with the others to begin their journey back to California.

And then, well, I went back to my life. Or at least I went back to a semblance of my former life. I still worked at the hotel in the mornings and the evenings. But newly inspired, I also returned to my dissertation. I called my doctoral advisor at the university in Florence to give him the news. He sounded pleased to hear I was back on track.

I also used my free time to meet regularly with Signora Vitarelli in the botanical garden. She sat on her usual bench with its view of the white lilies that are (as you may have heard) the national flower of Italy and the plot where we buried Mocho. Don't tell anyone because Bianca helped Mike, Monique, Fabrizio, and me sneak into the garden in the middle of the night to do it. Sofia's view also included her painting, which Professor Wilcox helped restore and move to a more prominent spot with a plaque identifying the artist and date.

 During our meetings, I helped Sofia get accustomed to her new dog. Whoever the mysterious person in the town was who found dogs for people provided Sofia with another furry footstool. I didn't ask, deciding it was a mystery I was happy to have remain a mystery. Dogs were just a part of life in Lacusara. While about the same size (as I said: footstool), the new dog was a 10-year-old corgi who toddled as he walked and had the biggest ears I'd ever seen. And I'm sure you will be glad to hear I no longer hid when Bianca walked into the garden, especially after I caught her sitting at Pietro's cafe with her new beau: Fabrizio. Good for them.

 Every Sunday night, I had dinner with Sofia and the rest of the Vitarelli family at the palazzo. Amelia, Gianpaolo, Teresa, and their daughters would come bearing an amazing array of food and wine. Professor Wilcox joined us the weeks he was in town cataloging Sofia's collection of paintings. We would eat and drink… and laugh. Sometimes I even brought a film for us all to watch, allowing me to view up close the collective joy and awe that movies can provide.

In short, I was re-entering society. It was a good life—a much better life than the one I had before the arrival of the group from UC Berkeley. But it lacked something incredibly important: Maggie.

Chapter Nineteen
MONIQUE

My time in Italy after the UC Berkeley trip ended took on a new hue for me. We managed to finish the trip in a way that pleased everyone—including (somehow) Clark. I also miraculously stayed out of hot water with both the alumni travel office and Scholarly Travel Adventures. They actually thanked me for taking over when Hilda disappeared (which she really did), never once asking the reason why. I will admit, though, that I found the whole experience rather taxing and decided to simplify my life by turning down requests to lecture to tour groups for the rest of the summer.

In a way, my days returned to a pattern similar to those before I became involved in the tours, with a few twists. I still rode my bike to the fresh market and down to the rugby field, and Mike and I still enjoyed our time in the equipment room—and in our own cottage, of course. On the weeks when it was appropriate, I got back out

♡ Monique ♡

on the field myself. Sometimes, Mike and I even went out and threw the ball around on our own or played with Fabrizio and other locals. We'd all end up at Bruno's bar wearing clothes stained with grass and dirt (and sometimes someone else's blood), and I felt a sense of camaraderie I hadn't known prior to stepping on the field. I pondered examining the phenomenon when I returned to Berkeley—once I finished the paper I was writing with Professor Wilcox on the mid-20th century conventions thwarting women artists (using Signora Vitarelli as our representative case), of course.

Or maybe I would save the thoughts on my newfound enjoyment of group sports for myself. There were quite possibly things in my life that didn't need to be studied academically. Like Mike. My Mike. Whenever I looked at him, I felt a love I never knew possible until I met him. It made no sense. We were as disparate as two people could be and yet… somehow not. Whatever we created together was more significant than the two of us, I suppose. That became even more apparent when, a few months after returning to Berkeley, I realized I hadn't had a period in a long time. Mike and I had never been particularly careful. Between passing 40 and our 4 years of almost constant commingling never even causing a scare, we recognized the odds of conception were not in our favor. We had even stopped pondering the concept after our original acknowledgment of the inherent pleasures in having a small creature to torment (isn't that what parenting entails?). Whatever biological functions the summer in Italy brought forth, it appeared they were fruitful. A drugstore test and subsequent visit to the doctor confirmed my suspicions.

After receiving the results and teaching my class, I walked down to the field the Cal rugby team used for their scrimmages. I sat in the bleachers on the sideline, watching the players fly back and forth down the field. When one of them took the legs out from under another, I clapped. Mike turned and saw me on the sidelines. He nodded and smiled.

"Go Cal, eh?"

I laughed. "Definitely."

"You want in?"

"Not today."

"You want to visit the equipment room?"

"No."

"No?" Mike looked worried and walked in my direction while still keeping half an eye on the action on the field. "Everything okay, babe?"

"Babe is kind of the operative word."

"Uh-huh," he said, still looking at his players. Then, as if suddenly realizing what I'd just said, turned back to me.

"I'm sorry. Babe?"

"Babe."

"Babe?"

I nodded. "Babe."

♡ Monique ♡

Mike ran over, picked me up in his big broad arms, and started twirling me around. "WE'RE GOING TO HAVE A BABY!" he started screaming.

The UC Berkeley rugby players, all as sweet (and built) as he was, ran in and surrounded us and started cheering. This new feeling of collective effervescence combined the exuberance of running down the field carrying the rugby ball with the communal solicitude that occurred when Mocho took his last breaths. I could only hope that my legs wouldn't be taken out from under me. We were, after all, bringing new life into this world. Having this new life revealed not long after Mocho's ended provided a soothing synchronicity to my lives in both Berkeley, California, and Bonvini, Italy. I couldn't wait until the following summer to share that new life with everyone in Italy.

Chapter Twenty
MAGGIE

When I left Italy, the most prevalent feeling I carried was not sadness but gratitude. Between meeting Emilio and the adventure we had uncovering Sofia Vitarelli's artworks—not to mention reuniting the Vitarelli family and giving Wilcox a new lease on life—I felt better than I had in a long time. Of course, that good mood was tempered a bit by the profound chaos of airline travel and not knowing if I would ever see Emilio again. But in general, I came home in a good place. I even decided to add a little life to my apartment. I finally walked into the flower shop on my street that I had passed by every day for years and picked out a few plants, including a white lily (the national flower of Italy, in case you haven't heard). I placed the lily on the mantle above my fireplace along with a small painting of the botanical garden Signora Vitarelli had slipped into my bag the last time I saw her. Together, they would remind me of Italy and help me to think better of people, even if I still felt most of them had a tendency to suck. (Hey, I'm working on it!)

I also decided to use my free time before the fall semester to check out the animal sanctuary Clark ran up in the Berkeley Hills. I was curious how this person who caused us so much consternation functioned in his native environment. When I arrived at the given address, I found a ranch-style house on a large lot that backed up to a preserve. I could already hear dogs barking as I exited my car. I walked through a side door labeled "Johnson Sanctuary Adoption Event" and found myself in a sea of both dogs and humanity (of the type looking to adopt a dog).

An older woman who radiated an earth-mother energy approached. "May I help you?" she asked.

"I'm looking for Clark. My name is Maggie McGrew…" I started.

"You're Maggie? Oh, thank you, thank you, thank you," the woman said, pulling me in for a humongous hug. "I'm Clark's mother, Phoebe."

"I'm sorry?" *Really? His mother? They could not be more different.*

"I run the sanctuary with Clark. Oh, he told me what a wonderful time he had on the trip."

"I'm sorry?" *Really? Clark said he enjoyed the trip?*

"He mentioned you might come by."

"I was curious to see the sanctuary." Okay, that part was true.

"I'll go find him," she said, dashing off before I could ask any of the questions running around in my head.

As I watched the dogs running here and there, it reminded me a little of the scavenger hunt that idiot had cooked up for the tech company (albeit with more fur and slobber involved). I couldn't help but start ascribing personality traits to each of the dogs and then to the people looking to adopt them. Before I could continue my little game, I saw Phoebe walking back with Clark, who had about a dozen dogs following him like he was the Pied Piper.

"Clark, good to see you."

"Professor McGrew," he growled. I swear the man growled at me again.

"See how happy he is?" Phoebe said before moving off to talk to a volunteer wearing a sanctuary t-shirt.

That's happy?

"Come to get a dog?" Clark asked.

"Not in a million years," I said. "But I will admit I'm curious as to how you match people up with the dogs."

Clark shrugged his shoulders. "We don't. We just let them choose."

"And how many people go home without a dog or take one that isn't a good fit?"

"More than we'd like!" Phoebe shouted from across the yard.

"Have you ever considered adding a little organization to the process?"

"In what way?" Clark asked.

I pointed to a single older gentleman, a family with young children, and an athletic-looking couple wearing tight-fitting exercise gear, all of whom appeared somewhat frozen and confused at the mass of canine energy milling about them. I then pointed to an older pug hiding off to the side, a young retriever maintaining very mellow energy amid all the chaos, and a border collie running in circles around everyone.

"Try those with them."

"On it!" Phoebe said, calling over some volunteers to help bring the dogs to meet the designated adopters. The pug folded into the older gentleman's arms, the retriever stood completely still (except for a wagging tail) while the kids petted him, and the border collie looked ready to run an obstacle course with the couple.

"You have to examine the body language," I said. "Not just the dogs. The people."

"People are not my strong suit," Clark said.

No shit, Sherlock, I thought, as Phoebe turned to give us a big thumbs up.

"You're good at this," he continued.

I shrugged. "I perform a similar service for tech companies in Silicon Valley."

"Want to help out on our adoption days? We hold them two afternoons a week."

Are you crazy? Hang out with you and your dogs two afternoons a week? "Do you pay what they pay?" I asked.

"We do not, in fact, pay at all."

"Okay, I'm in."

Yeah, I didn't really need much cajoling, especially as it gave me a great idea for a new book on group dynamics using dog breeds. You know that famous picture of the dogs playing poker? Think of it transferred to a corporate board. Brilliant, right? Plus, the rescue gig would help counteract teaching entitled undergrads and working with even more entitled tech companies. As Clark and I discussed the details, a ridiculously cute floppy-eared terrier mix walked over and plopped down on my shoe.

"Looks like you have a new friend," Clark said.

"I do not have a new friend," I said oh-so-quickly.

"Look at that," Phoebe called as she walked back toward us. "You're the first person he's warmed up to, Maggie!"

"Oh, don't say that," I whined (just a bit).

"Sorry, Maggie. He picked you," Clark said.

"Did he, though?"

Phoebe and Clark both nodded emphatically. "Yeah, he did."

"You have to examine the body language. Not just the people. The dogs," Clark said with an expression verging on a smile. I should have growled at him.

"You can always foster him," Phoebe suggested as she and Clark exchanged glances. "Seriously, if you could take him home for a day or two, that would be a huge help. He could really use a break from the chaos of the other dogs."

"I suppose he could come home with me," I said to the little guy, who did look rattled at all the commotion. "Just for the night."

Famous last words, right? So, yeah, I got a dog. The little guy—named, not particularly originally, "Lil Guy"—had spiky gray, white, and black fur and looked to be a mix of a million breeds. In short, he would never make the promenade of purebreds in Lacusara. Not only that, but he was messy (and you know how I feel about messy!). Hairs on my furniture. Stupid dog toys strewn all about. Okay, so yes, I bought the stupid dog toys, but he was the one who insisted on flinging them here and there. But he was darn cute and easygoing and a pretty good snuggle pup, especially on those nights when I missed a certain someone.

I probably shouldn't admit this, but I even became one of those annoying people who takes their dog everywhere. This included the weekly coffee dates I had with Kathy at Caffe Strada, where Lil Guy and I would greet Professor Gabriel and his Great Dane before sitting at our usual table.

"You heard the news about Monique and Mike, I suppose?" Kathy started the week after we learned Monique was pregnant.

"I did. I'm really happy for them."

"Me, too. Me, too," Kathy said, looking at Lil Guy and giving him a pet. "New life is a good thing, don't you think?"

"I do."

"I'll have you all over for dinner soon," Kathy said. She paused before continuing, "Any word from Emilio?"

"We talk. Text."

"How is he doing?"

"Good… Back working on his dissertation and helping Signora Vitarelli with her latest dog."

"Another Pekinese?"

"Corgi."

"Did Emilio discover who keeps the dog ledger? Assuming there really is one…"

"Still a mystery."

"And no talk of…"

"None."

"Okay, I won't push."

"Or War Council him?"

Kathy laughed. "Or War Council him. Cross my heart. Although I can tell you it's saving my life."

"The War Council?"

"Helping other people. That's what it does, you know, Maggie. You created a good thing there, even if you aren't involved in it anymore."

I smiled and, for the first time, just said, "Thanks. I appreciate that. And you."

Kathy looked at her watch. "I'd better go. Tonight's my night with the kids."

"You know, whenever you're ready, I'm happy to give Brian a good old-fashioned smack across the face. Or you could have Monique tackle him. That's what she does now."

"Oh, I know," Kathy said, laughing. "And I appreciate that. But you know what? I'm okay. Today, I'm okay. Thanks." Kathy gave my hand a quick squeeze and took off, and Lil Guy and I headed home.

The following week, I received a text from Kathy saying she was running late for our Caffe Strada date. *Of course, she is,* I thought, *but, hey, at least she took the time to let me know.* Progress. For all of us. Lil Guy and I continued our walk to Caffe Strada, expecting to find the usual sea of anonymous faces and an empty table. But as I turned the corner, there he was, sitting at the table, with the warm eyes and the brown hair he used those glorious fingers to push off his face. I felt a big ole "it's good to be alive" smile forming on my face. Finally, someone was waiting for me at Caffe Strada.

"*Buona sera,* Margherita," Emilio said, standing as Lil Guy and I reached the table.

"*Buona sera*, Emilio."

"And who is this?"

"This is Lil Guy. Lil Guy, this is Emilio."

Emilio bent down and gave Lil Guy a pet on the head. Lil Guy responded by sitting on his shoe. When Emilio stood back up, we took a moment to stare at each other wearing shit-eating grins (that's the technical term) on our faces.

"So…" Emilio finally said. "My Ph.D. advisor suggested that the University of California, Berkeley, might be the ideal place for me to finish my dissertation."

"Is it now?"

"I mean, what better place to study awe … and joy," he said, looking at me with that beautiful smile of his.

"No better…" I said. "Well, there is Italy."

"There is Italy. But you are not in Italy. And that makes Berkeley preferable," Emilio said, looking down at Lil Guy and then back up to meet my eyes. "Here is what I am thinking: Although a wise person once told me that people…"

We both said "suck" together, smiling.

"…there are certain persons in this world who do not. The truth is they make life quite wonderful. And it is with these people that I think I should be."

Emilio put his hand out. I took it and laced my fingers in his as he pulled me in for a kiss. And it was gooood. When I finally pulled back and opened my eyes, I saw Kathy standing off to the side, smiling. I nodded in Emilio's direction, and Kathy used her hands to indicate I should go.

"Let's go home," I said to Emilio.

"I would like that."

Emilio held my hand and together we—Emilio, Lil Guy, and I—walked back to my apartment. I smiled what I knew was same smile Signora Vitarelli had in her painting. Joy. When you find something or someone you love, that's the feeling. Absolute joy.

So, yeah, my trip to Italy was messy. But there are times in your life when messy is okay. More than okay, even. Necessary.

THE END

Book Club Questions

1. Maggie starts the book by saying that Italy was messier than she expected. What do you think she means by that?

2. In the first chapter, Maggie says she thinks "people suck." Is this something you agree with (and why)? Does her opinion change?

3. Describe Monique's life during the summers she spends in Italy. How does it change when she gets involved with the university-related tours of Italy?

4. How does Emilio end up bartending at the Hotel Botanico? What is his view of the tourists who come through the hotel?

5. Of the three characters telling the story—Maggie, Monique, and Emilio—who do you relate to the most? Least? Why?

6. Would you want to take a trip to Italy like the one described in the book (before or after Monique starts making changes)? What would your ideal trip to Italy look like?

7. Emilio and Maggie discover a secret in the botanical garden. What did you think of their sleuthing? Was the artist they uncovered who you thought it would be? Why?

8. Professor Wilcox is described as a pompous bore when Maggie learns he will be on the trip. Is this a fair assessment? Does his summer in Italy change his demeanor?

9. Monique and Maggie decide to "War Council" Professor Wilcox and Hilda, the tour director. How does it go?

10. There are a number of budding romances in the book. Which was your favorite new couple? Which surprised you the most?

11. Emilio makes a lot of spritzes (Aperol and otherwise) in the book. Which kind of spritz is your favorite?

12. A lot of things happen in both Italy and Berkeley at the end of the book. What did you find most surprising or were you happiest about?

Acknowledgements

The Italy depicted in *The Italy Affair* is real. It is also fictional. By that I mean that while everything depicted in the book can be found in Italy, the elements have gone through the blender of my imagination to create the story. For this reason, instead of using actual cities, I created fictional amalgams. In other words, do not attempt to search for the towns of Bonvini, Lacusara or Verniciara (or the artist Paolo Luciano). They don't exist, even though everything in them can be found somewhere in Italy. If you would like to know more—like where you can find all the dogs—feel free to contact me via my website: annshepphird.com.

My thanks, as always, to all who helped bring this book to life, especially Jill Bastian and Luana Presta, whose feedback on early drafts improved the book immeasurably. Thanks also to my editor, Jen Paquette, and to Laura Mita, Beau Lake, Valerie Willis, Erika Lance, and Jordan Weiner.

About the Author

In her 20+ years as a writer and editor, Ann Shepphird has covered everything from travel and sports to gardening and food to design and transportation for a variety of publications.

Now Ann is tackling her favorite topics—mysteries and rom-coms—for 4 Horsemen Publications. The Destination Murder Mysteries combine Ann's experiences as a travel journalist with her stint working for a private investigator while the University Chronicles series of rom-coms are based on her days as a college-level communications instructor.

Ann lives in Santa Monica, California, with her long-time partner, Jeff, and their furry companions Melody and Winnie. When she's not writing, Ann is most likely to be found on a tennis court or in her garden.

**Discover more at
4HorsemenPublications.com**

10% off using HORSEMEN10

Milton Keynes UK
Ingram Content Group UK Ltd.
UKHW041700121224
3635UKWH00019B/48